MINNIE & DAISY

BEST FRIENDS FOREVER

D0517013

CALGARY PUBLIC LIBRARY

OCT 2016

Graphic Novels Available from
PAPERCUT Z

Graphic Novel #1
"Prilla's Talent"

Graphic Novel #2
"Tinker Bell and the
Wings of Rani"

Graphic Novel #3
"Tinker Bell and the
Day of the Dragon"

Graphic Novel #4
"Tinker Bell
to the Rescue"

Graphic Novel #5
"Tinker Bell and the
Pirate Adventure"

Graphic Novel #6
"A Present
for Tinker Bell"

Graphic Novel #7
"Tinker Bell the
Perfect Fairy"

Graphic Novel #8
"Tinker Bell and her
Stories for a Rainy Day"

Graphic Novel #9
"Tinker Bell and
her Magical Arrival"

Graphic Novel #10
"Tinker Bell and
the Lucky Rainbow"

Graphic Novel #11
"Tinker Bell and the
Most Precious Gift"

Graphic Novel #12
"Tinker Bell and the
Lost Treasure"

Graphic Novel #13
"Tinker Bell and the
Pixie Hollow Games"

Graphic Novel #14
"Tinker Bell and
Blaze"

**Tinker Bell
and the Great
Fairy Rescue**

Graphic Novel #15
"Tinker Bell and the
Secret of the Wings"

Graphic Novel #16
"Tinker Bell and the
Pirate Fairy"

Graphic Novel #17
"Tinker Bell and the
Legend of the NeverBeast"

DISNEY FAIRIES graphic novels are available in paperback for $7.99 each;
in hardcover for $12.99 each except #5, $6.99PB, $10.99HC. #6-14 are $7.99PB $11.99HC.
#15 – 18 are $7.99PB $12.99HC.
Tinker Bell and the Great Fairy Rescue is $9.99 in hardcover only.
Available at booksellers everywhere.

See more at papercutz.com

Or you can order from us: Please add $4.00 for postage and handling for first book, and add $1.00 for each additional book.
Please make check payable to NBM Publishing. Send to: Papercutz, 160 Broadway, Suite 700, East Wing, New York, NY 10038
or call 800 886 1223 (9-6 EST M-F) MC-Visa-Amex accepted.

Graphic Novel #18
"Tinker Bell and her
Magical Friends"

Disney

Minnie & Daisy

Best Friends Forever

PAPERCUTZ
New York

Contents

DISNEY GRAPHIC NOVELS #
"Minnie & Dais
Dawn K. Guzzo - Design/Productio
Jeff Whitman - Production Coordinato
Robert V. Conte - Edito
Bethany Bryan - Associate Edito
Jim Salicru
Editor-in-Chie

ISBN: 9781629914718 Paperback editio
ISBN: 9781629914725 Hardcover editio
Copyright © 2016 by Disney Enterprises, In
All rights reserved

Printed in Kore
July 2016 by We SP Co., LTD
79-29, Soraji-r
Paju-Si, Gyeonggi-do, 1086

Papercutz books may be purchased for business or promotional use
For information on bulk purchases please contac
Macmillan Corporate and Premium Sales Department at (800) 221-7945 x544

Distributed by Macmillan
First Papercutz Printing

Disney MINNIE & DAISY BEST FRIENDS FOREVER

The Field of Fashion!

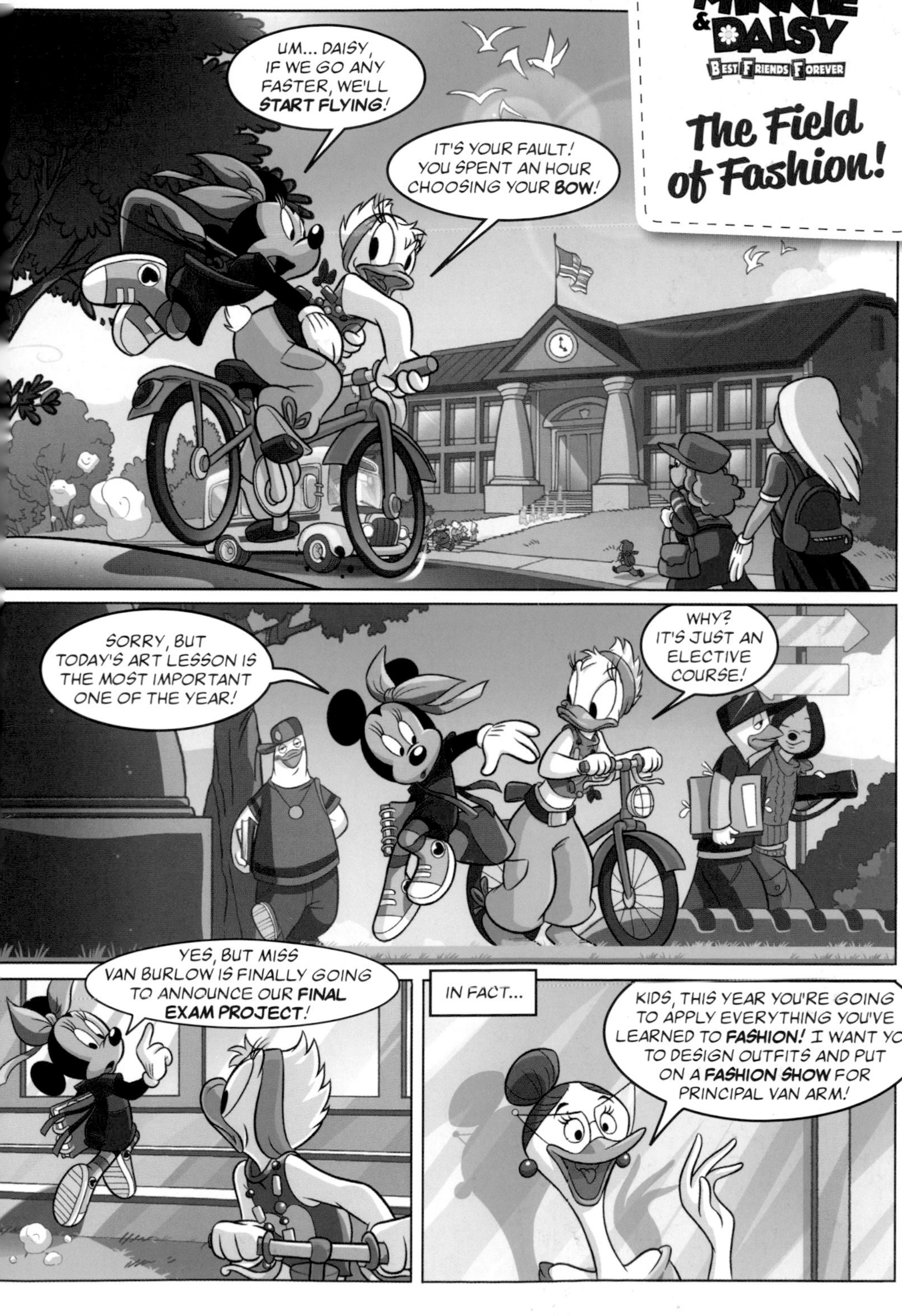
UM... DAISY, IF WE GO ANY FASTER, WE'LL START FLYING!
IT'S YOUR FAULT! YOU SPENT AN HOUR CHOOSING YOUR BOW!
SORRY, BUT TODAY'S ART LESSON IS THE MOST IMPORTANT ONE OF THE YEAR!
WHY? IT'S JUST AN ELECTIVE COURSE!
YES, BUT MISS VAN BURLOW IS FINALLY GOING TO ANNOUNCE OUR FINAL EXAM PROJECT!
IN FACT...
KIDS, THIS YEAR YOU'RE GOING TO APPLY EVERYTHING YOU'VE LEARNED TO FASHION! I WANT YOU TO DESIGN OUTFITS AND PUT ON A FASHION SHOW FOR PRINCIPAL VAN ARM!

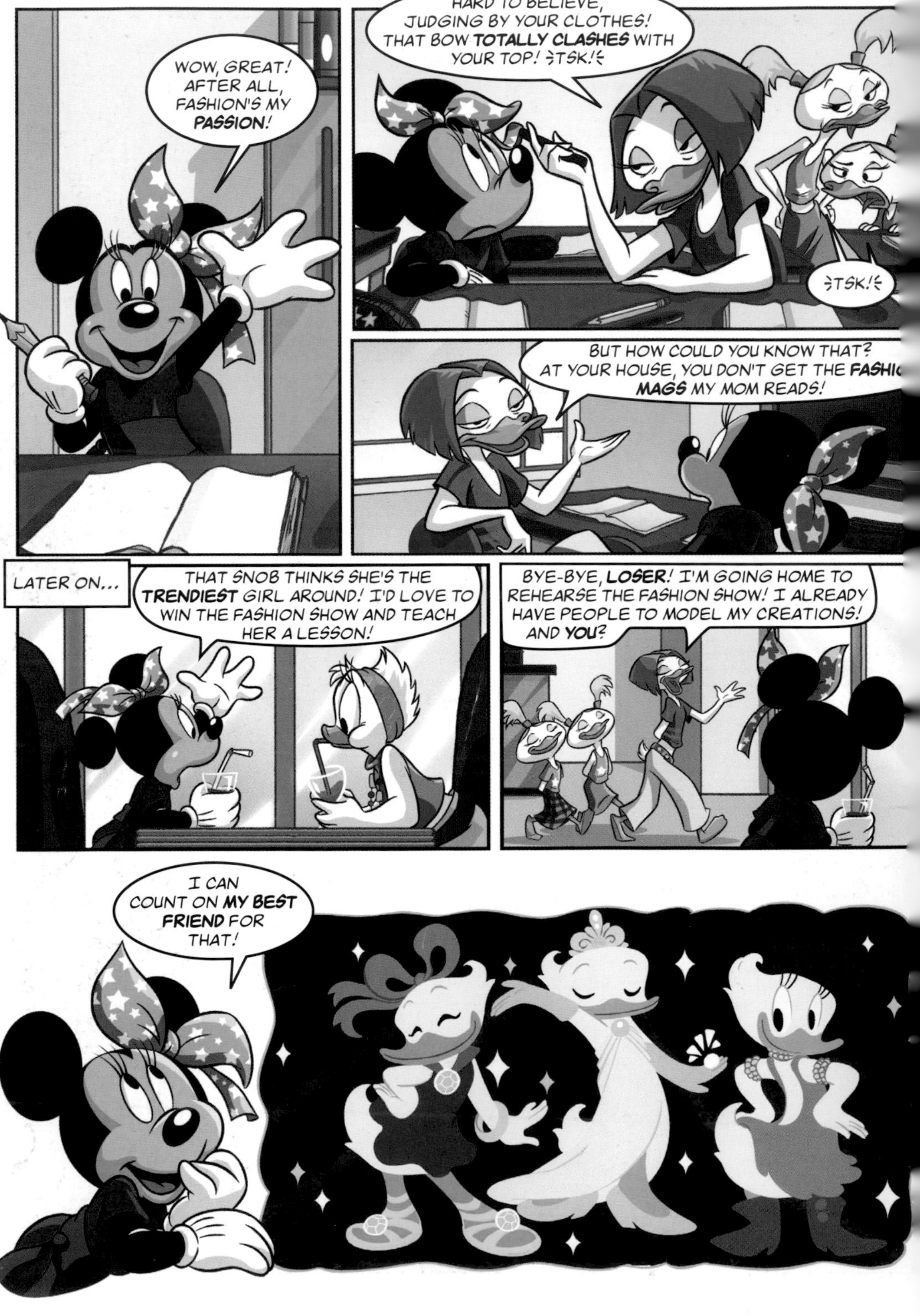
WOW, GREAT! AFTER ALL, FASHION'S MY PASSION!
HARD TO BELIEVE, JUDGING BY YOUR CLOTHES! THAT BOW TOTALLY CLASHES WITH YOUR TOP! TSK!
TSK!
BUT HOW COULD YOU KNOW THAT? AT YOUR HOUSE, YOU DON'T GET THE FASHIO MAGS MY MOM READS!
LATER ON...
THAT SNOB THINKS SHE'S THE TRENDIEST GIRL AROUND! I'D LOVE TO WIN THE FASHION SHOW AND TEACH HER A LESSON!
BYE-BYE, LOSER! I'M GOING HOME TO REHEARSE THE FASHION SHOW! I ALREADY HAVE PEOPLE TO MODEL MY CREATIONS! AND YOU?
I CAN COUNT ON MY BEST FRIEND FOR THAT!

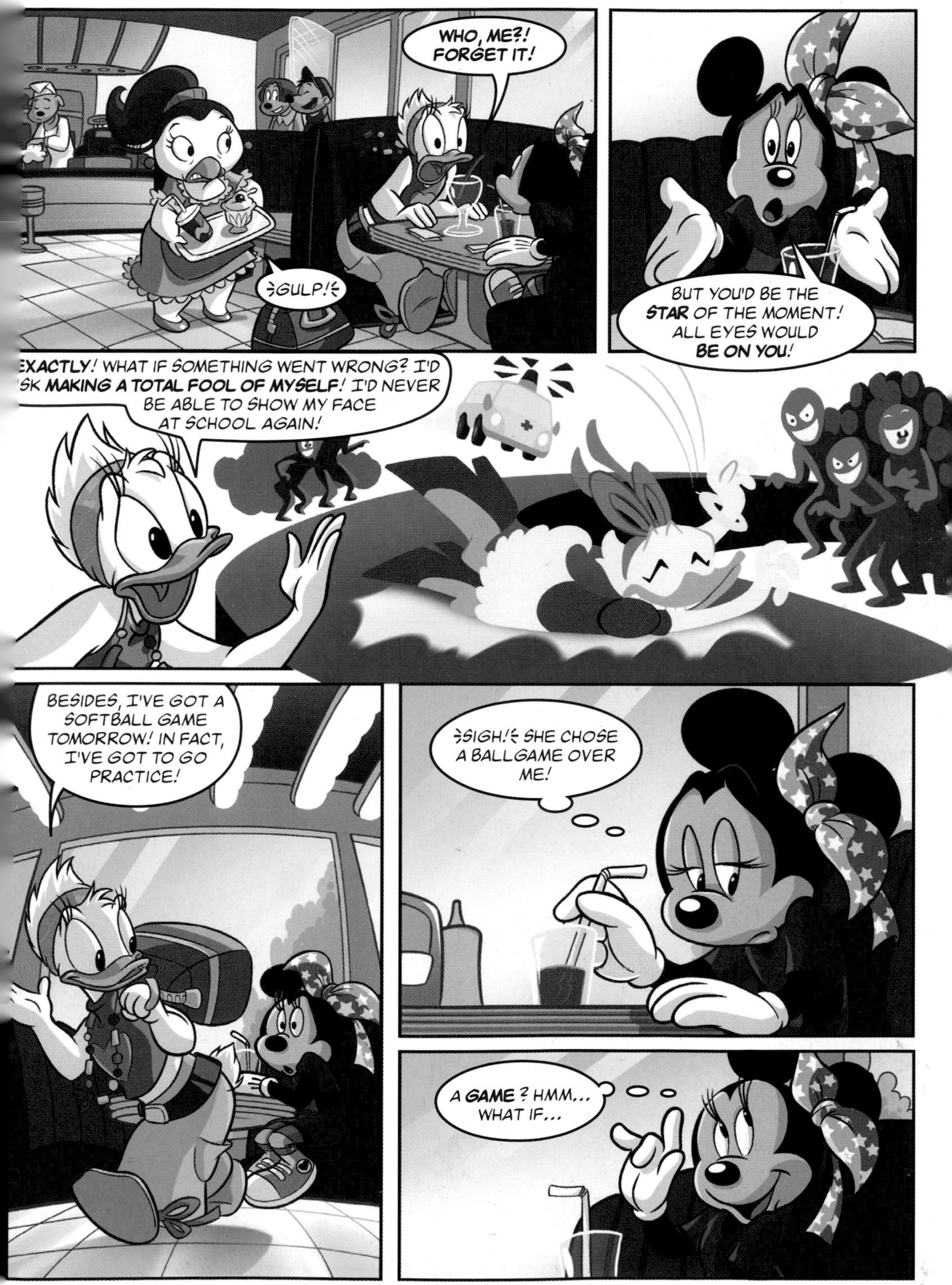
WHO, ME?! FORGET IT!
GULP!
BUT YOU'D BE THE STAR OF THE MOMENT! ALL EYES WOULD BE ON YOU!
EXACTLY! WHAT IF SOMETHING WENT WRONG? I'D SK MAKING A TOTAL FOOL OF MYSELF! I'D NEVER BE ABLE TO SHOW MY FACE AT SCHOOL AGAIN!
BESIDES, I'VE GOT A SOFTBALL GAME TOMORROW! IN FACT, I'VE GOT TO GO PRACTICE!
SIGH! SHE CHOSE A BALLGAME OVER ME!
A GAME? HMM... WHAT IF...

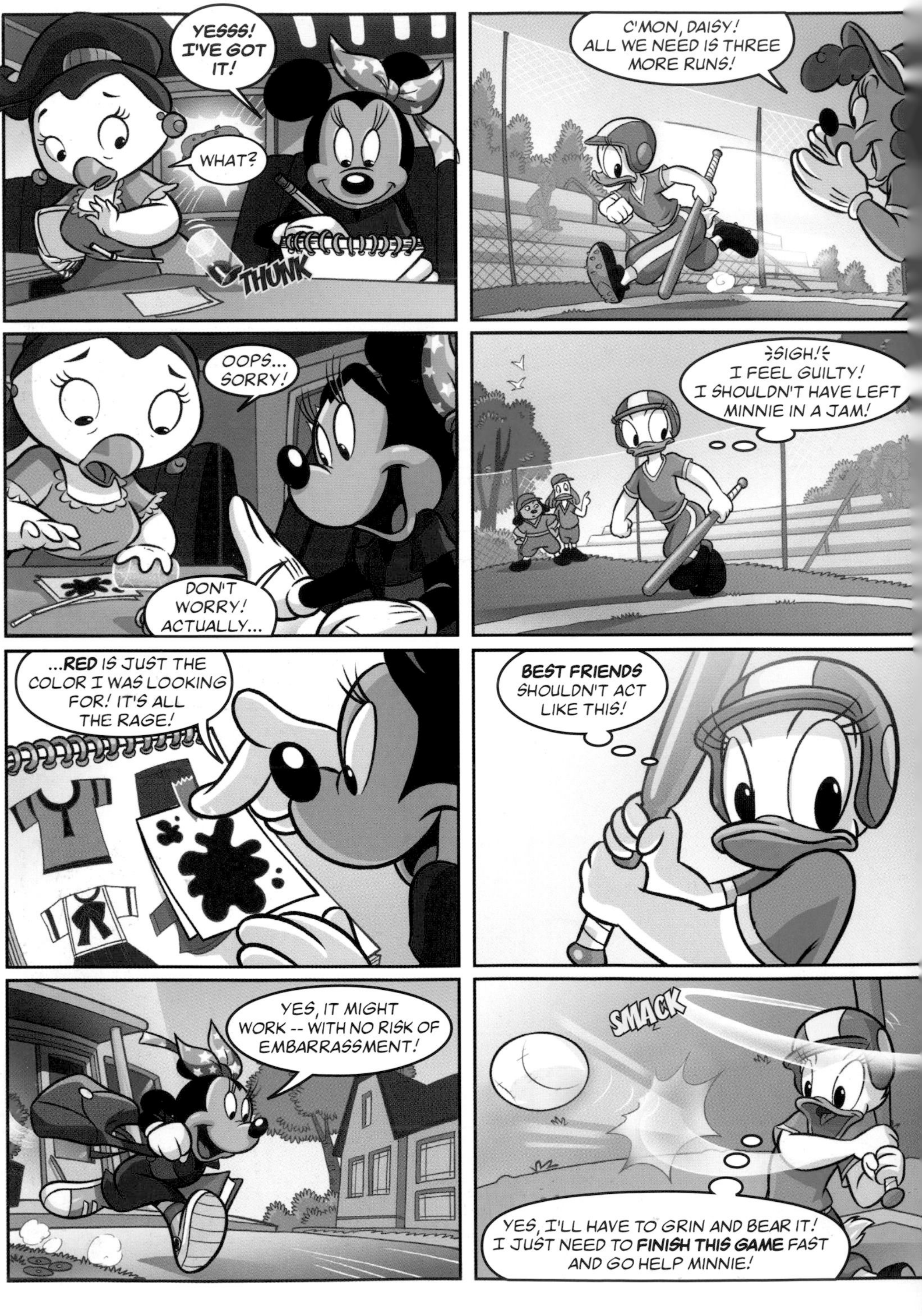

YESSS! I'VE GOT IT!
WHAT?
THUNK
C'MON, DAISY! ALL WE NEED IS THREE MORE RUNS!
OOPS... SORRY!
DON'T WORRY! ACTUALLY...
SIGH! I FEEL GUILTY! I SHOULDN'T HAVE LEFT MINNIE IN A JAM!
...RED IS JUST THE COLOR I WAS LOOKING FOR! IT'S ALL THE RAGE!
BEST FRIENDS SHOULDN'T ACT LIKE THIS!
YES, IT MIGHT WORK -- WITH NO RISK OF EMBARRASSMENT!
SMACK
YES, I'LL HAVE TO GRIN AND BEAR IT! I JUST NEED TO FINISH THIS GAME FAST AND GO HELP MINNIE!

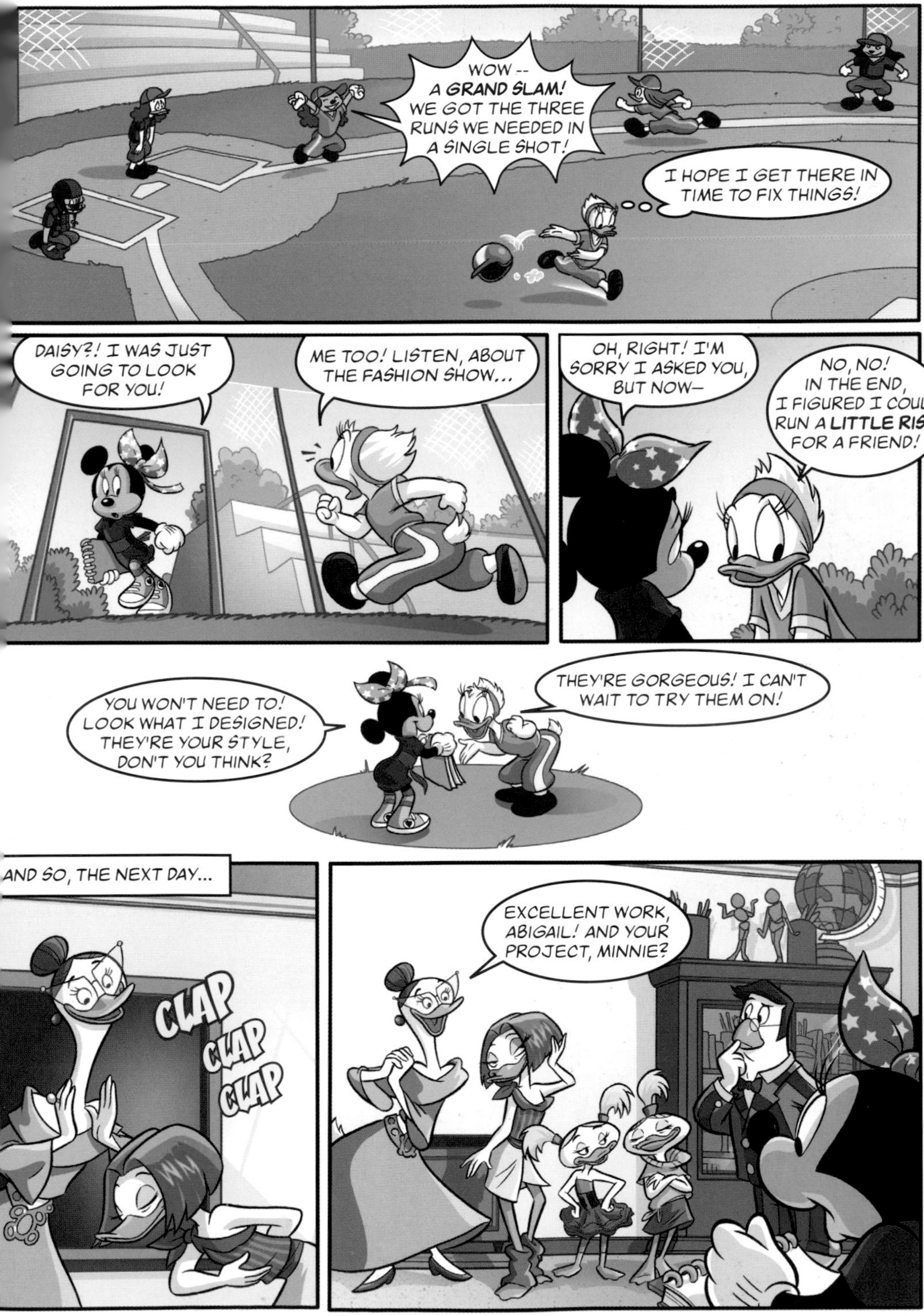
WOW -- A GRAND SLAM! WE GOT THE THREE RUNS WE NEEDED IN A SINGLE SHOT!
I HOPE I GET THERE IN TIME TO FIX THINGS!
DAISY?! I WAS JUST GOING TO LOOK FOR YOU!
ME TOO! LISTEN, ABOUT THE FASHION SHOW...
OH, RIGHT! I'M SORRY I ASKED YOU, BUT NOW—
NO, NO! IN THE END, I FIGURED I COULD RUN A LITTLE RISK FOR A FRIEND!
YOU WON'T NEED TO! LOOK WHAT I DESIGNED! THEY'RE YOUR STYLE, DON'T YOU THINK?
THEY'RE GORGEOUS! I CAN'T WAIT TO TRY THEM ON!
AND SO, THE NEXT DAY...
CLAP CLAP CLAP
EXCELLENT WORK, ABIGAIL! AND YOUR PROJECT, MINNIE?

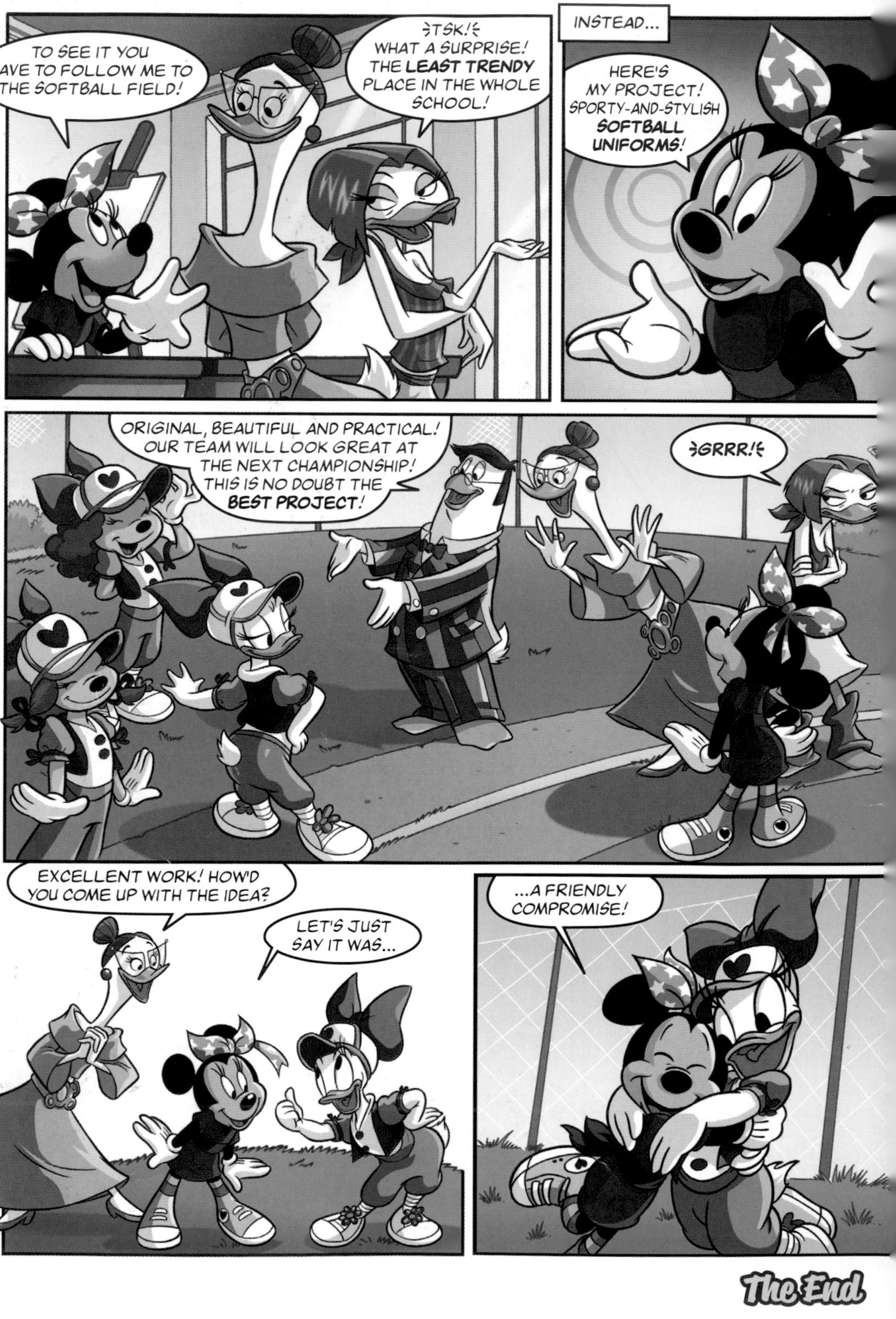
TO SEE IT YOU HAVE TO FOLLOW ME TO THE SOFTBALL FIELD!
TSK! WHAT A SURPRISE! THE **LEAST TRENDY** PLACE IN THE WHOLE SCHOOL!
INSTEAD...
HERE'S MY PROJECT! SPORTY-AND-STYLISH **SOFTBALL UNIFORMS**!
ORIGINAL, BEAUTIFUL AND PRACTICAL! OUR TEAM WILL LOOK GREAT AT THE NEXT CHAMPIONSHIP! THIS IS NO DOUBT THE **BEST PROJECT**!
GRRR!
EXCELLENT WORK! HOW'D YOU COME UP WITH THE IDEA?
LET'S JUST SAY IT WAS...
...A FRIENDLY COMPROMISE!
The End

Disney Minnie & Daisy Best Friends Forever

Much Ado About Juliet

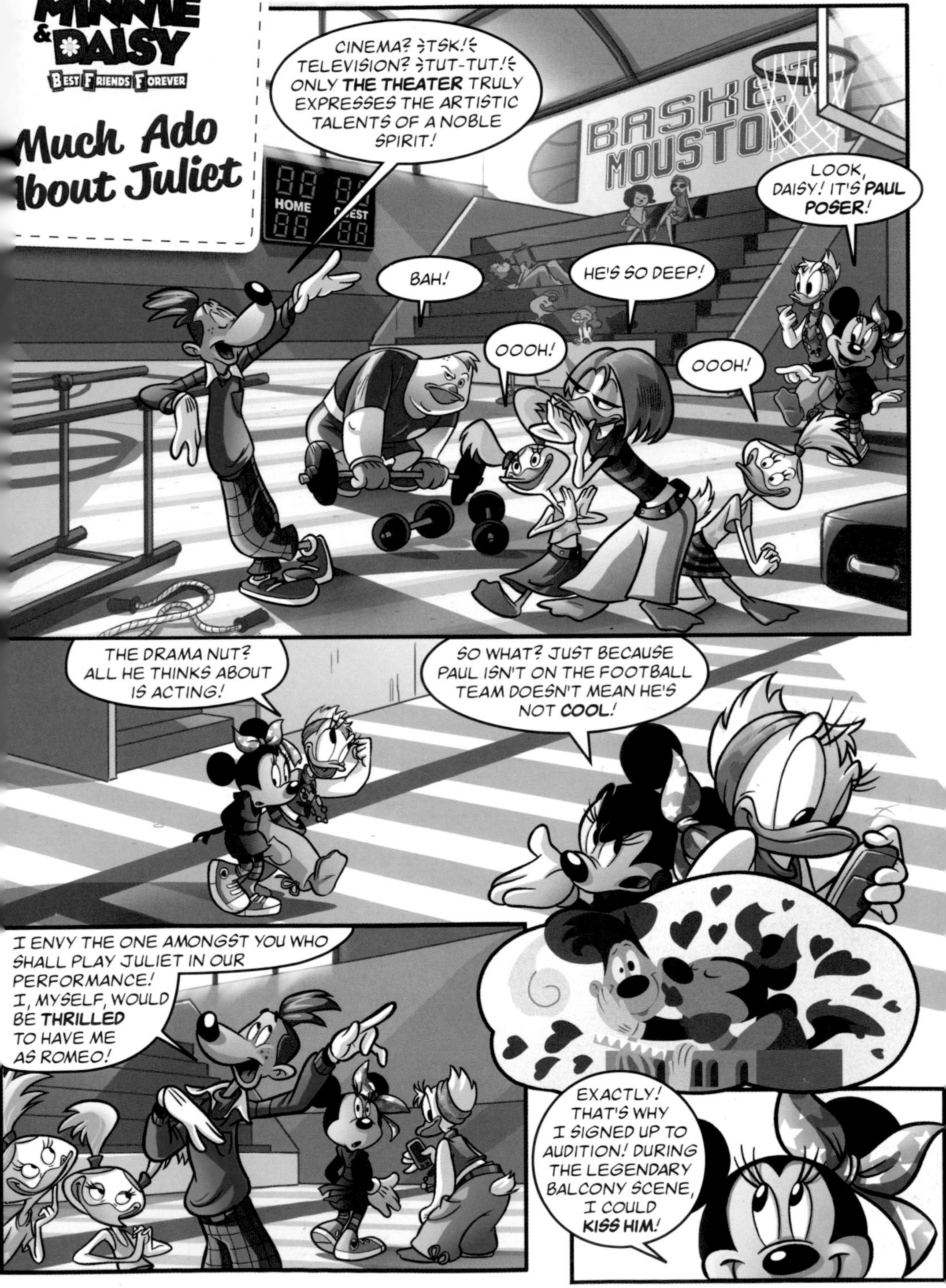
CINEMA? TSK! TELEVISION? TUT-TUT! ONLY **THE THEATER** TRULY EXPRESSES THE ARTISTIC TALENTS OF A NOBLE SPIRIT!
BAH!
OOOH!
HE'S SO DEEP!
OOOH!
LOOK, DAISY! IT'S **PAUL POSER**!
BASKET MOUSTON
HOME GUEST
THE DRAMA NUT? ALL HE THINKS ABOUT IS ACTING!
SO WHAT? JUST BECAUSE PAUL ISN'T ON THE FOOTBALL TEAM DOESN'T MEAN HE'S NOT **COOL**!
I ENVY THE ONE AMONGST YOU WHO SHALL PLAY JULIET IN OUR PERFORMANCE! I, MYSELF, WOULD BE **THRILLED** TO HAVE ME AS ROMEO!
EXACTLY! THAT'S WHY I SIGNED UP TO AUDITION! DURING THE LEGENDARY BALCONY SCENE, I COULD **KISS HIM**!

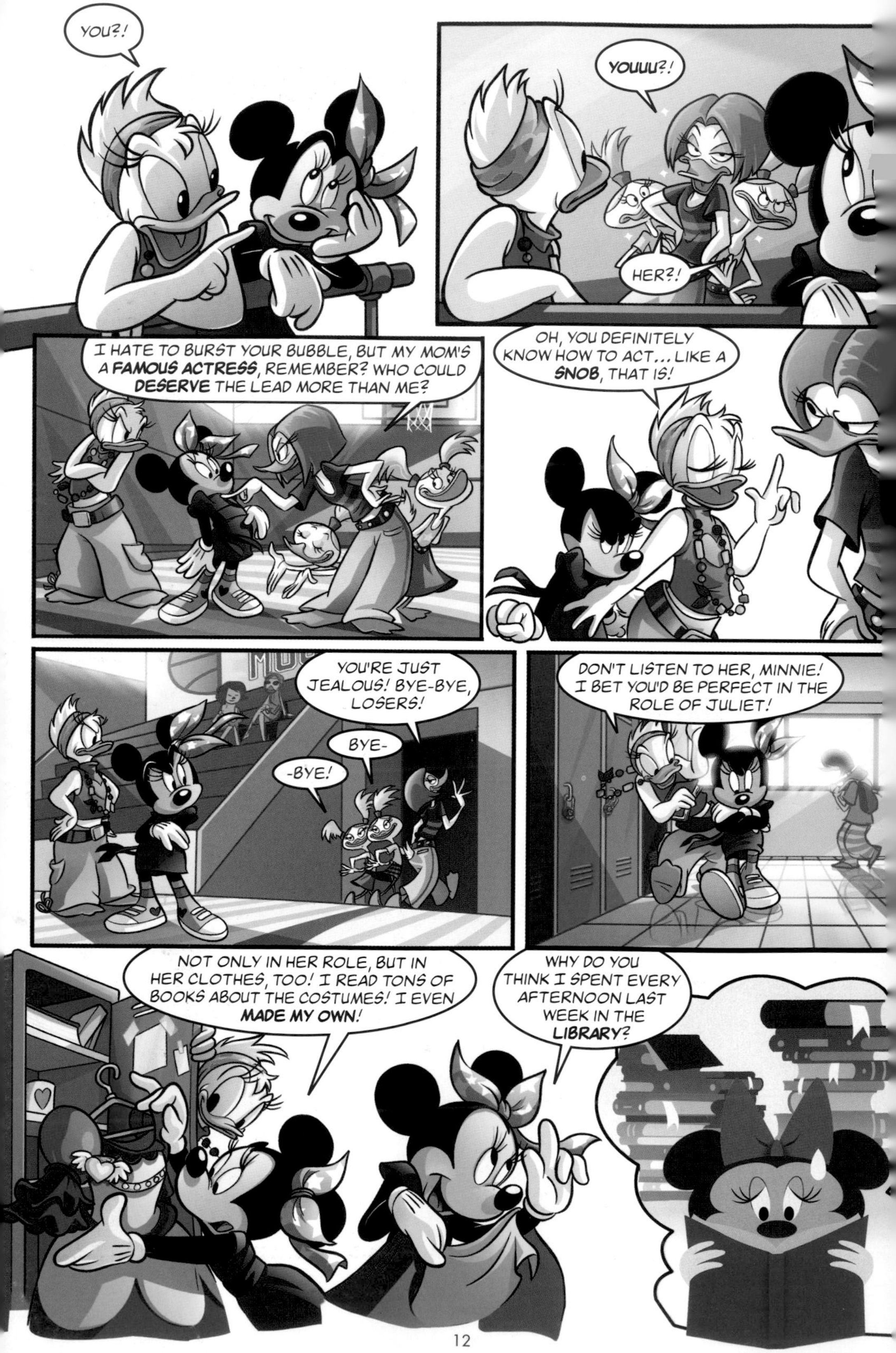
YOU?!
YOUUU?!
HER?!
I HATE TO BURST YOUR BUBBLE, BUT MY MOM'S A **FAMOUS ACTRESS**, REMEMBER? WHO COULD **DESERVE** THE LEAD MORE THAN ME?
OH, YOU DEFINITELY KNOW HOW TO ACT... LIKE A **SNOB**, THAT IS!
YOU'RE JUST JEALOUS! BYE-BYE, LOSERS!
BYE-
-BYE!
DON'T LISTEN TO HER, MINNIE! I BET YOU'D BE PERFECT IN THE ROLE OF JULIET!
NOT ONLY IN HER ROLE, BUT IN HER CLOTHES, TOO! I READ TONS OF BOOKS ABOUT THE COSTUMES! I EVEN **MADE MY OWN**!
WHY DO YOU THINK I SPENT EVERY AFTERNOON LAST WEEK IN THE **LIBRARY**?

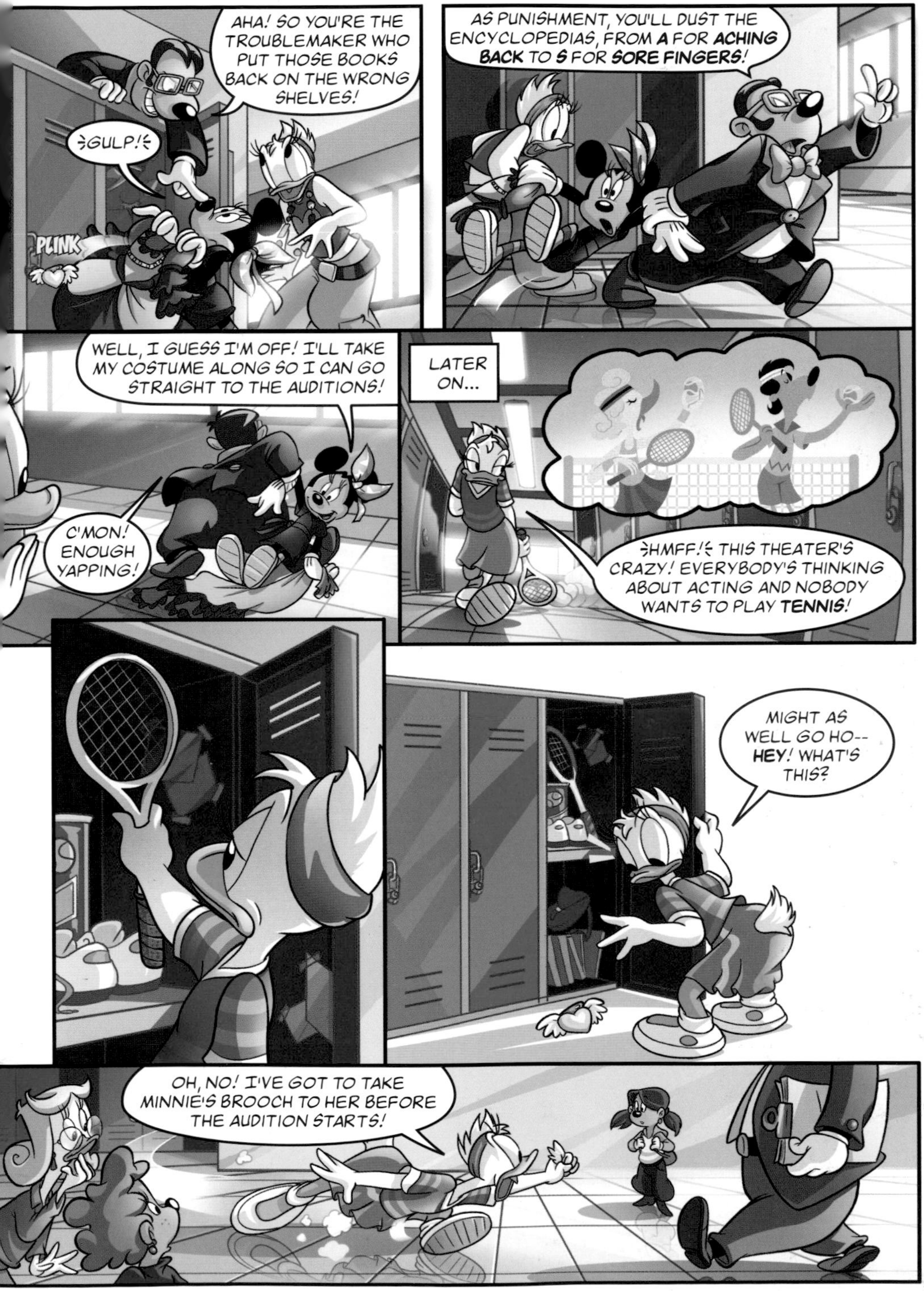
AHA! SO YOU'RE THE TROUBLEMAKER WHO PUT THOSE BOOKS BACK ON THE WRONG SHELVES!
GULP!
PLINK
AS PUNISHMENT, YOU'LL DUST THE ENCYCLOPEDIAS, FROM **A** FOR **ACHING BACK** TO **S** FOR **SORE FINGERS**!
WELL, I GUESS I'M OFF! I'LL TAKE MY COSTUME ALONG SO I CAN GO STRAIGHT TO THE AUDITIONS!
C'MON! ENOUGH YAPPING!
LATER ON...
HMFF! THIS THEATER'S CRAZY! EVERYBODY'S THINKING ABOUT ACTING AND NOBODY WANTS TO PLAY **TENNIS**!
MIGHT AS WELL GO HO-- **HEY**! WHAT'S THIS?
OH, NO! I'VE GOT TO TAKE MINNIE'S BROOCH TO HER BEFORE THE AUDITION STARTS!

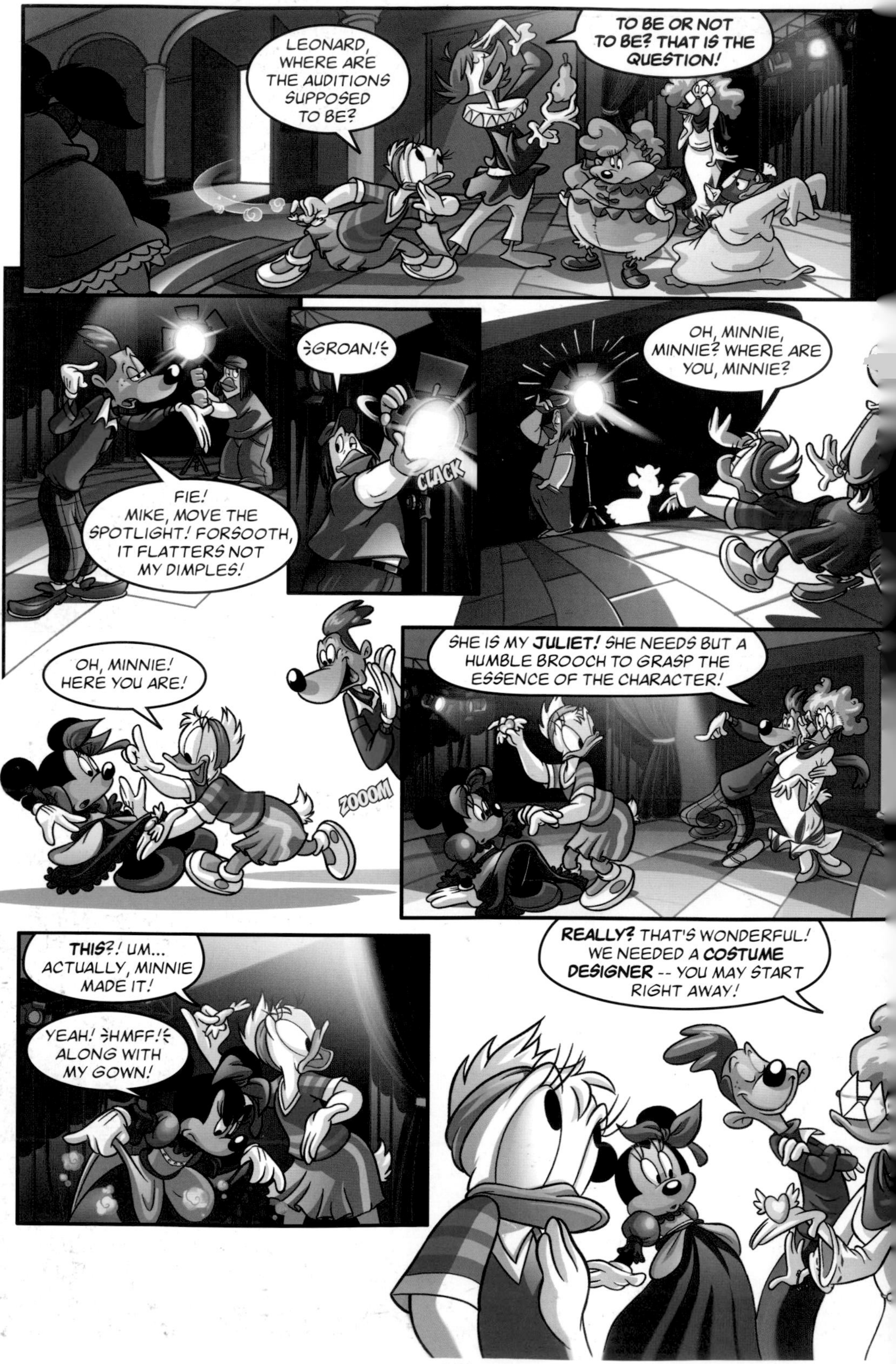
LEONARD, WHERE ARE THE AUDITIONS SUPPOSED TO BE?
TO BE OR NOT TO BE? THAT IS THE QUESTION!
FIE! MIKE, MOVE THE SPOTLIGHT! FORSOOTH, IT FLATTERS NOT MY DIMPLES!
GROAN!
CLACK
OH, MINNIE, MINNIE? WHERE ARE YOU, MINNIE?
OH, MINNIE! HERE YOU ARE!
ZOOOM
SHE IS MY JULIET! SHE NEEDS BUT A HUMBLE BROOCH TO GRASP THE ESSENCE OF THE CHARACTER!
THIS?! UM... ACTUALLY, MINNIE MADE IT!
YEAH! HMFF! ALONG WITH MY GOWN!
REALLY? THAT'S WONDERFUL! WE NEEDED A COSTUME DESIGNER -- YOU MAY START RIGHT AWAY!

COSTUME DESIGNER?! NOOO!

YOU WANT HER TO DESIGN MY DRESS FOR THE PLAY? ɨUGH!ɨ

ɨBLEAH!ɨ

THEN DON'T AUDITION! BESIDES, THE BEST PART YOU COULD GET NOW IS SCULLERY MAID!

ARISE, FAIR JULIET!

DAISY!

AS YOU MUST IMMERSE YOURSELF IN YOUR CHARACTER, HENCEFORTH I SHALL CALL YOU JULIET!

ɨPEHɨ, WHATEVER...

GONE, COSTUME DESIGNER! EXEUNT ALL! MAKE WAY FOR THE ARTISTES!

BUT I LEARNED THE LINES BY HEART! I COULD RECITE THEM BACKWARDS!

ɨWHIMPER!ɨ

WELL, YOU CAN BE DAISY'S UNDERSTUDY! IF SHE MISSES THE PLAY, YOU'LL REPLACE HER!

SO...

ROMEO, ROMEO! WHEREFORE ART THOU, ROMEO?

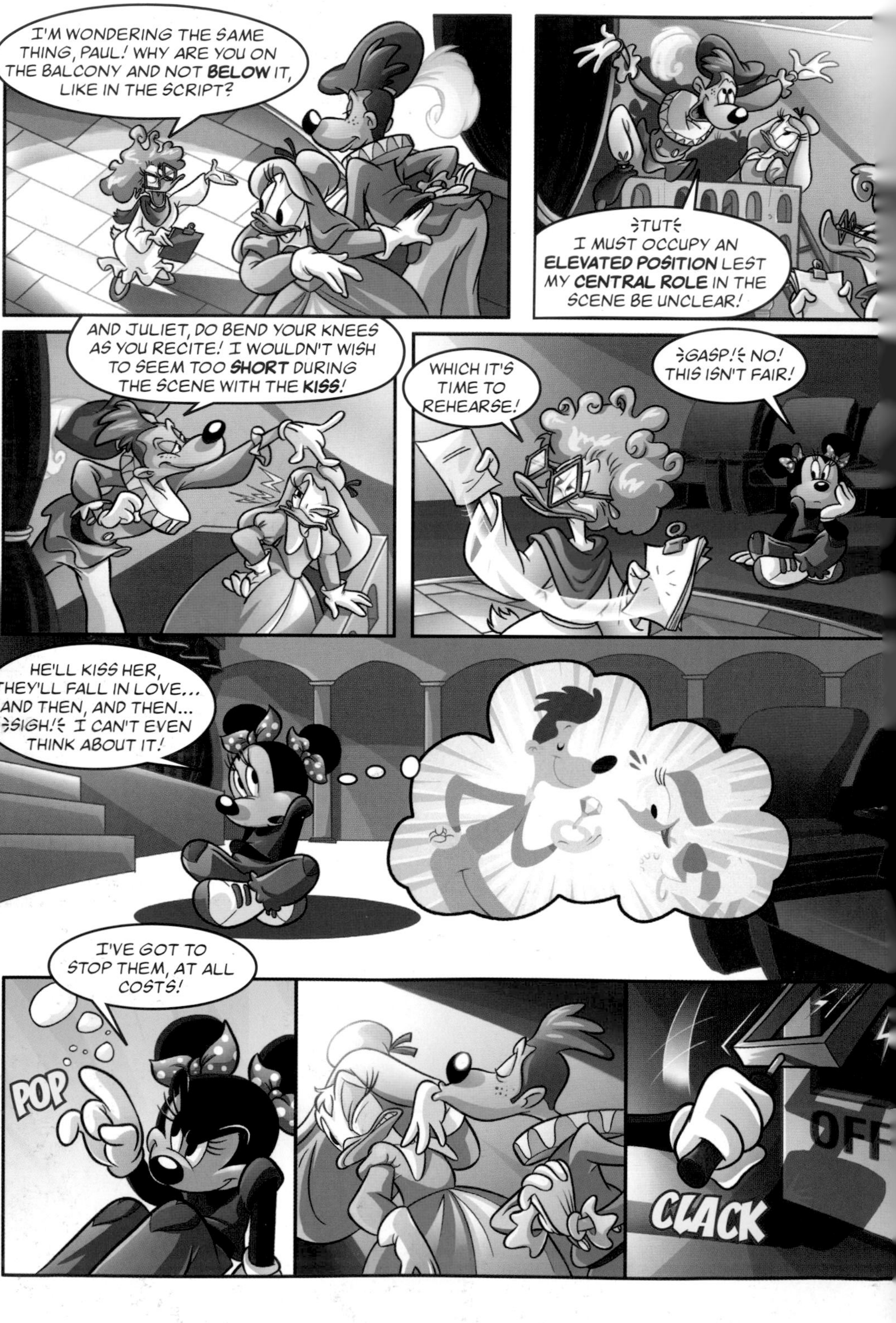

I'M WONDERING THE SAME THING, PAUL! WHY ARE YOU ON THE BALCONY AND NOT BELOW IT, LIKE IN THE SCRIPT?
TUT
I MUST OCCUPY AN ELEVATED POSITION LEST MY CENTRAL ROLE IN THE SCENE BE UNCLEAR!
AND JULIET, DO BEND YOUR KNEES AS YOU RECITE! I WOULDN'T WISH TO SEEM TOO SHORT DURING THE SCENE WITH THE KISS!
WHICH IT'S TIME TO REHEARSE!
GASP! NO! THIS ISN'T FAIR!
HE'LL KISS HER, THEY'LL FALL IN LOVE... AND THEN, AND THEN... SIGH! I CAN'T EVEN THINK ABOUT IT!
I'VE GOT TO STOP THEM, AT ALL COSTS!
POP
OFF
CLACK

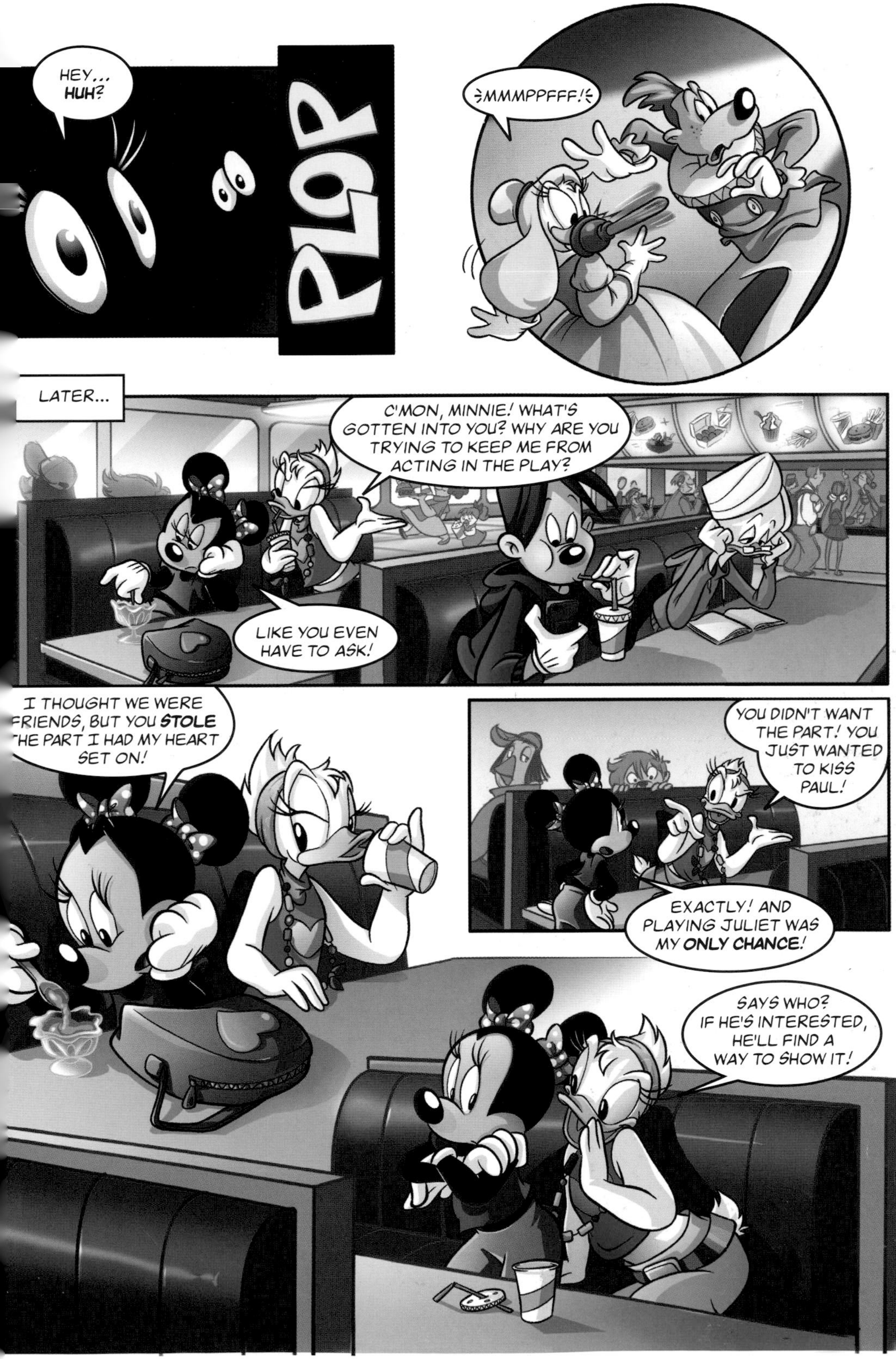

HEY... HUH?
PLOP
MMMPPFFF!
LATER...
C'MON, MINNIE! WHAT'S GOTTEN INTO YOU? WHY ARE YOU TRYING TO KEEP ME FROM ACTING IN THE PLAY?
LIKE YOU EVEN HAVE TO ASK!
I THOUGHT WE WERE FRIENDS, BUT YOU STOLE THE PART I HAD MY HEART SET ON!
YOU DIDN'T WANT THE PART! YOU JUST WANTED TO KISS PAUL!
EXACTLY! AND PLAYING JULIET WAS MY ONLY CHANCE!
SAYS WHO? IF HE'S INTERESTED, HE'LL FIND A WAY TO SHOW IT!

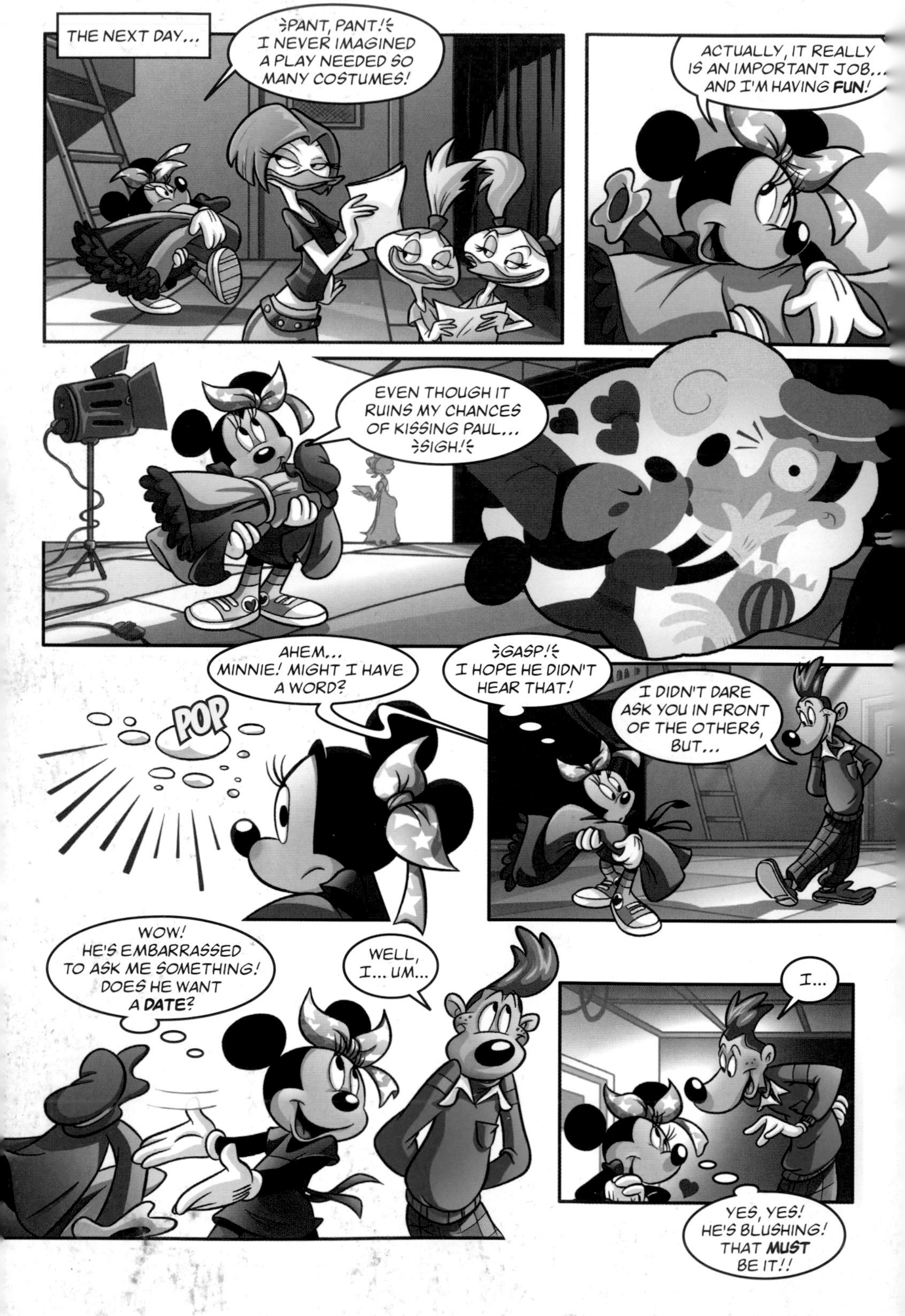
THE NEXT DAY...
⊰PANT, PANT!⊱ I NEVER IMAGINED A PLAY NEEDED SO MANY COSTUMES!
ACTUALLY, IT REALLY IS AN IMPORTANT JOB... AND I'M HAVING **FUN**!
EVEN THOUGH IT RUINS MY CHANCES OF KISSING PAUL... ⊰SIGH!⊱
AHEM... MINNIE! MIGHT I HAVE A WORD?
POP
⊰GASP!⊱ I HOPE HE DIDN'T HEAR THAT!
I DIDN'T DARE ASK YOU IN FRONT OF THE OTHERS, BUT...
WOW! HE'S EMBARRASSED TO ASK ME SOMETHING! DOES HE WANT A **DATE**?
WELL, I... UM...
I...
YES, YES! HE'S BLUSHING! THAT **MUST** BE IT!!

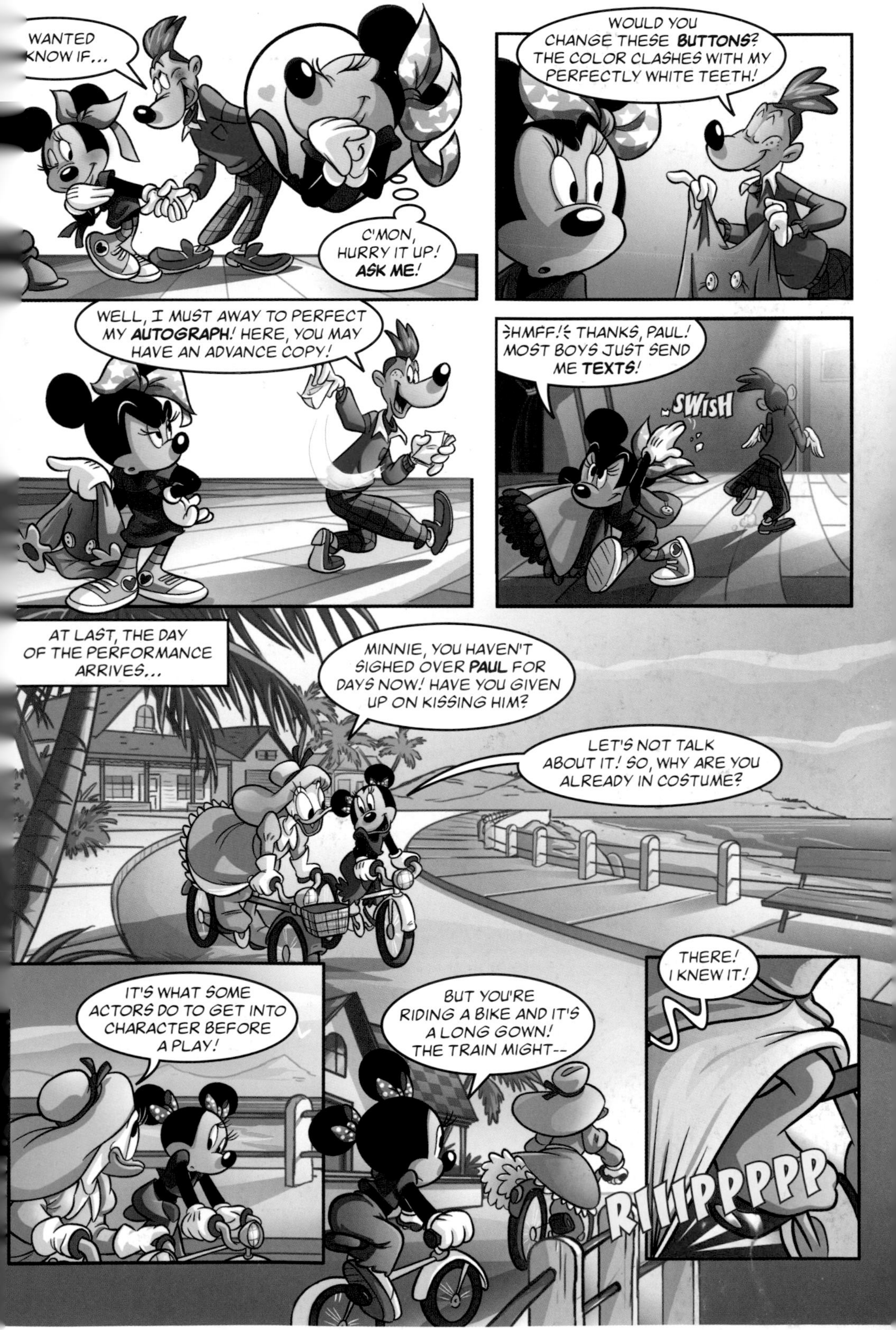
WANTED
KNOW IF...
C'MON, HURRY IT UP! ASK ME!
WOULD YOU CHANGE THESE BUTTONS? THE COLOR CLASHES WITH MY PERFECTLY WHITE TEETH!
WELL, I MUST AWAY TO PERFECT MY AUTOGRAPH! HERE, YOU MAY HAVE AN ADVANCE COPY!
HMFF! THANKS, PAUL! MOST BOYS JUST SEND ME TEXTS!
SWISH
AT LAST, THE DAY OF THE PERFORMANCE ARRIVES...
MINNIE, YOU HAVEN'T SIGHED OVER PAUL FOR DAYS NOW! HAVE YOU GIVEN UP ON KISSING HIM?
LET'S NOT TALK ABOUT IT! SO, WHY ARE YOU ALREADY IN COSTUME?
IT'S WHAT SOME ACTORS DO TO GET INTO CHARACTER BEFORE A PLAY!
BUT YOU'RE RIDING A BIKE AND IT'S A LONG GOWN! THE TRAIN MIGHT--
THERE! I KNEW IT!
RIIIPPPPP

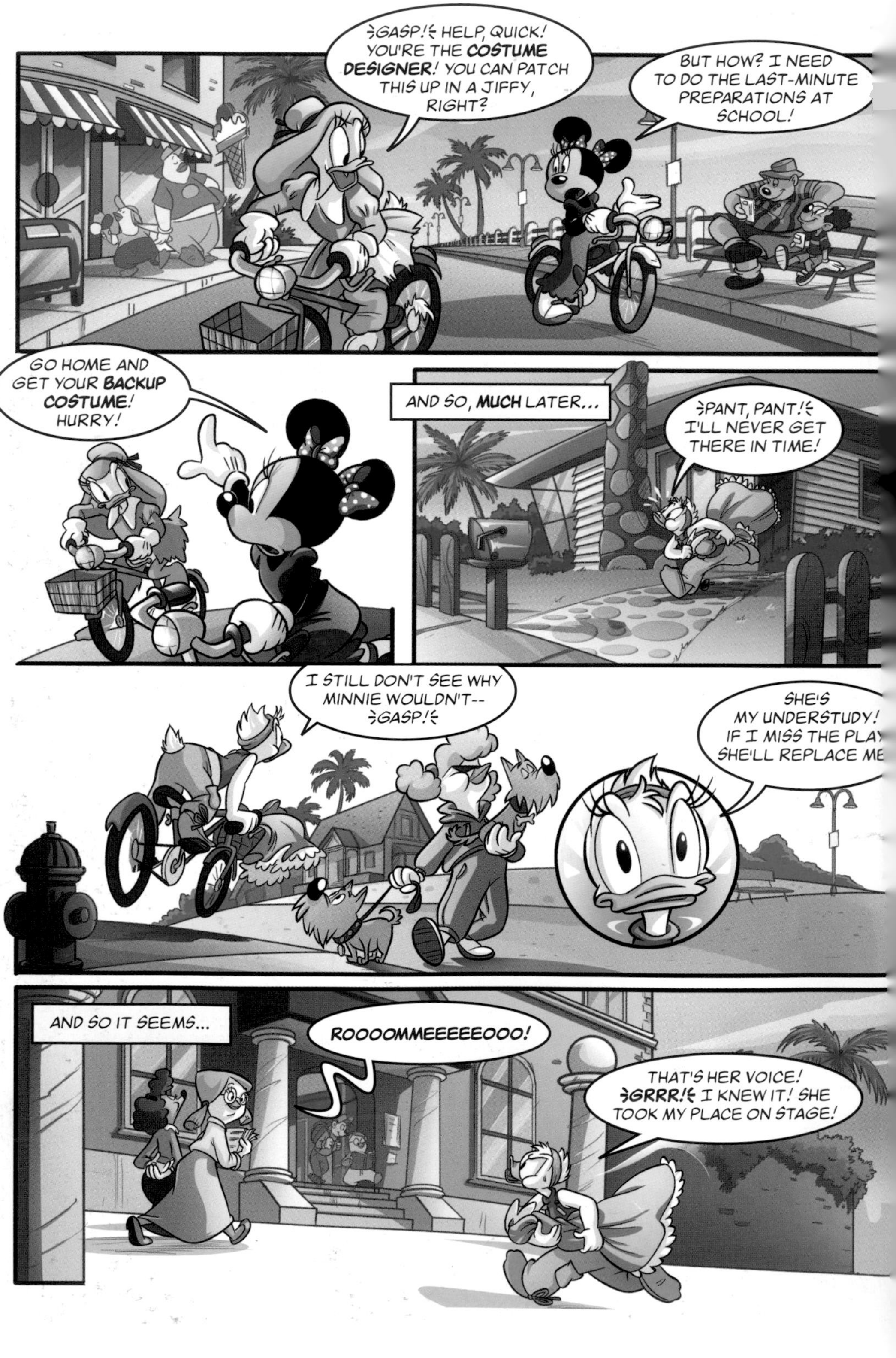

⋟GASP!⋞ HELP, QUICK! YOU'RE THE **COSTUME DESIGNER**! YOU CAN PATCH THIS UP IN A JIFFY, RIGHT?
BUT HOW? I NEED TO DO THE LAST-MINUTE PREPARATIONS AT SCHOOL!
GO HOME AND GET YOUR **BACKUP COSTUME**! HURRY!
AND SO, **MUCH** LATER...
⋟PANT, PANT!⋞ I'LL NEVER GET THERE IN TIME!
I STILL DON'T SEE WHY MINNIE WOULDN'T-- ⋟GASP!⋞
SHE'S MY UNDERSTUDY! IF I MISS THE PLA SHE'LL REPLACE ME
AND SO IT SEEMS...
ROOOOMMEEEEEOOO!
THAT'S HER VOICE! **⋟GRRR!⋞** I KNEW IT! SHE TOOK MY PLACE ON STAGE!

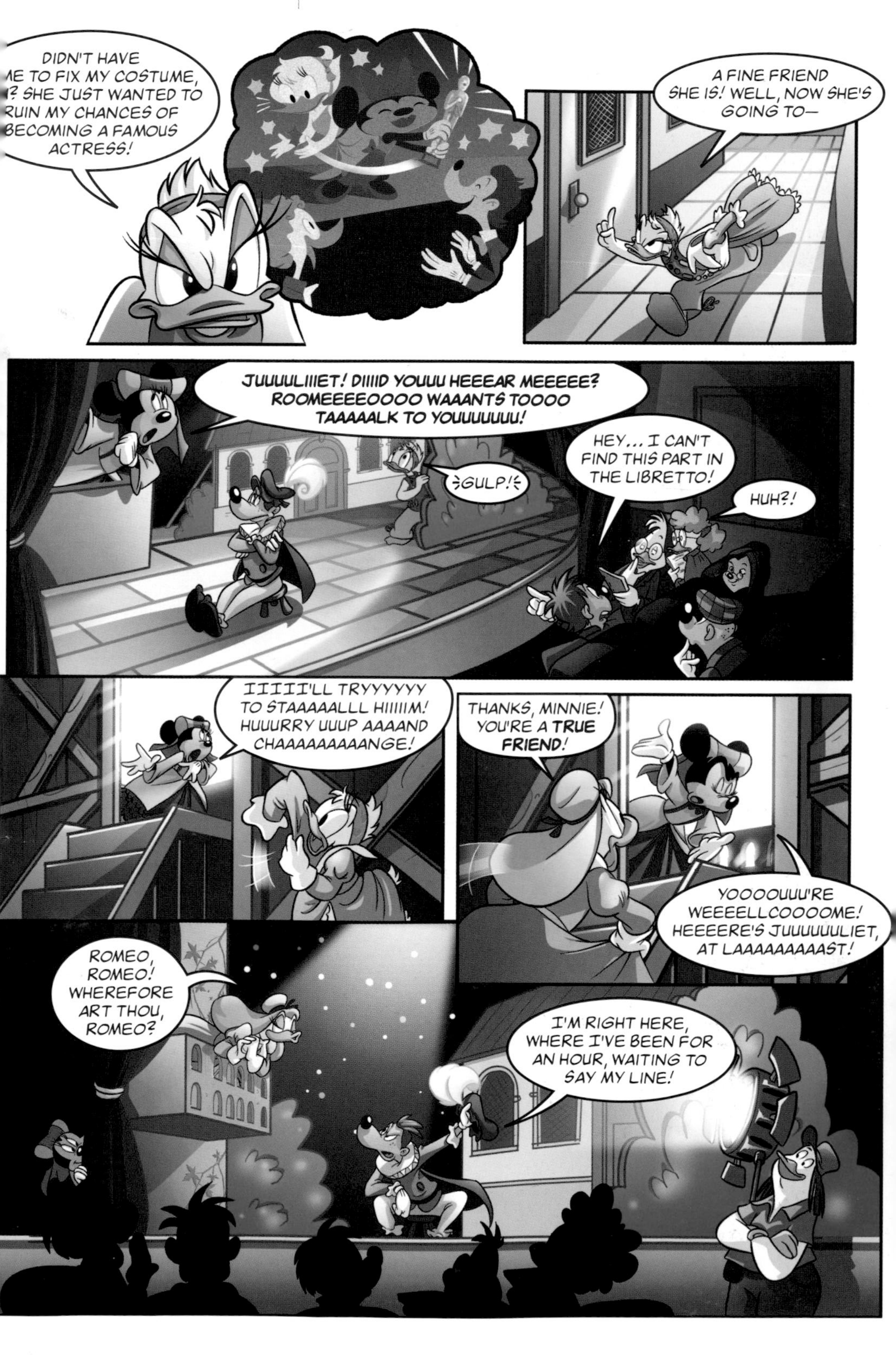

DIDN'T HAVE ME TO FIX MY COSTUME, ? SHE JUST WANTED TO RUIN MY CHANCES OF BECOMING A FAMOUS ACTRESS!
A FINE FRIEND SHE IS! WELL, NOW SHE'S GOING TO—
JUUUULIIIET! DIIIID YOUUU HEEEAR MEEEEE? ROOMEEEEOOOO WAAANTS TOOOO TAAAAALK TO YOUUUUUUU!
GULP!
HEY... I CAN'T FIND THIS PART IN THE LIBRETTO!
HUH?!
IIIII'LL TRYYYYYY TO STAAAAALLL HIIIIIM! HUUURRY UUUP AAAAND CHAAAAAAAAANGE!
THANKS, MINNIE! YOU'RE A **TRUE FRIEND**!
YOOOOUUU'RE WEEEELLCOOOOME! HEEEERE'S JUUUUUULIET, AT LAAAAAAAAAST!
ROMEO, ROMEO! WHEREFORE ART THOU, ROMEO?
I'M RIGHT HERE, WHERE I'VE BEEN FOR AN HOUR, WAITING TO SAY MY LINE!

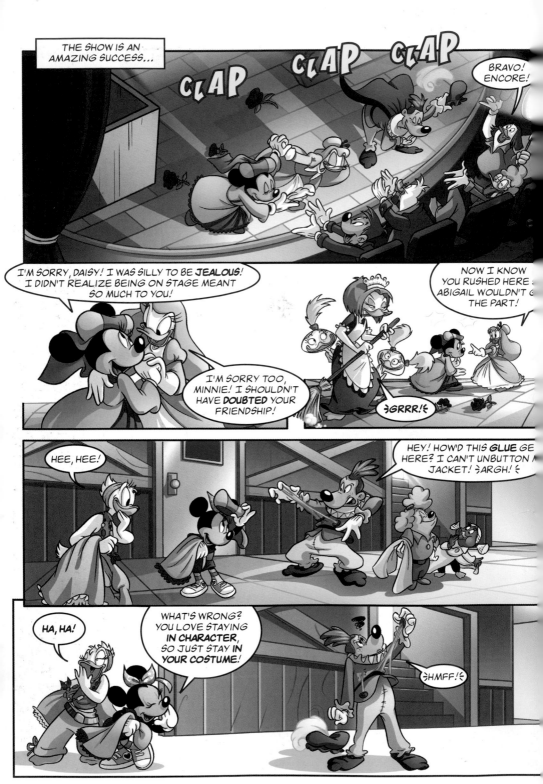

THE SHOW IS AN AMAZING SUCCESS...

CLAP CLAP CLAP

BRAVO! ENCORE!

I'M SORRY, DAISY! I WAS SILLY TO BE **JEALOUS**! I DIDN'T REALIZE BEING ON STAGE MEANT SO MUCH TO YOU!

I'M SORRY TOO, MINNIE! I SHOULDN'T HAVE **DOUBTED** YOUR FRIENDSHIP!

NOW I KNOW YOU RUSHED HERE ABIGAIL WOULDN'T THE PART!

ʒGRRR!ʃ

HEE, HEE!

HEY! HOW'D THIS **GLUE** GE HERE? I CAN'T UNBUTTON JACKET! ʒARGH!ʃ

HA, HA!

WHAT'S WRONG? YOU LOVE STAYING **IN CHARACTER**, SO JUST STAY **IN** YOUR COSTUME!

ʒHMFF!ʃ

The End

22

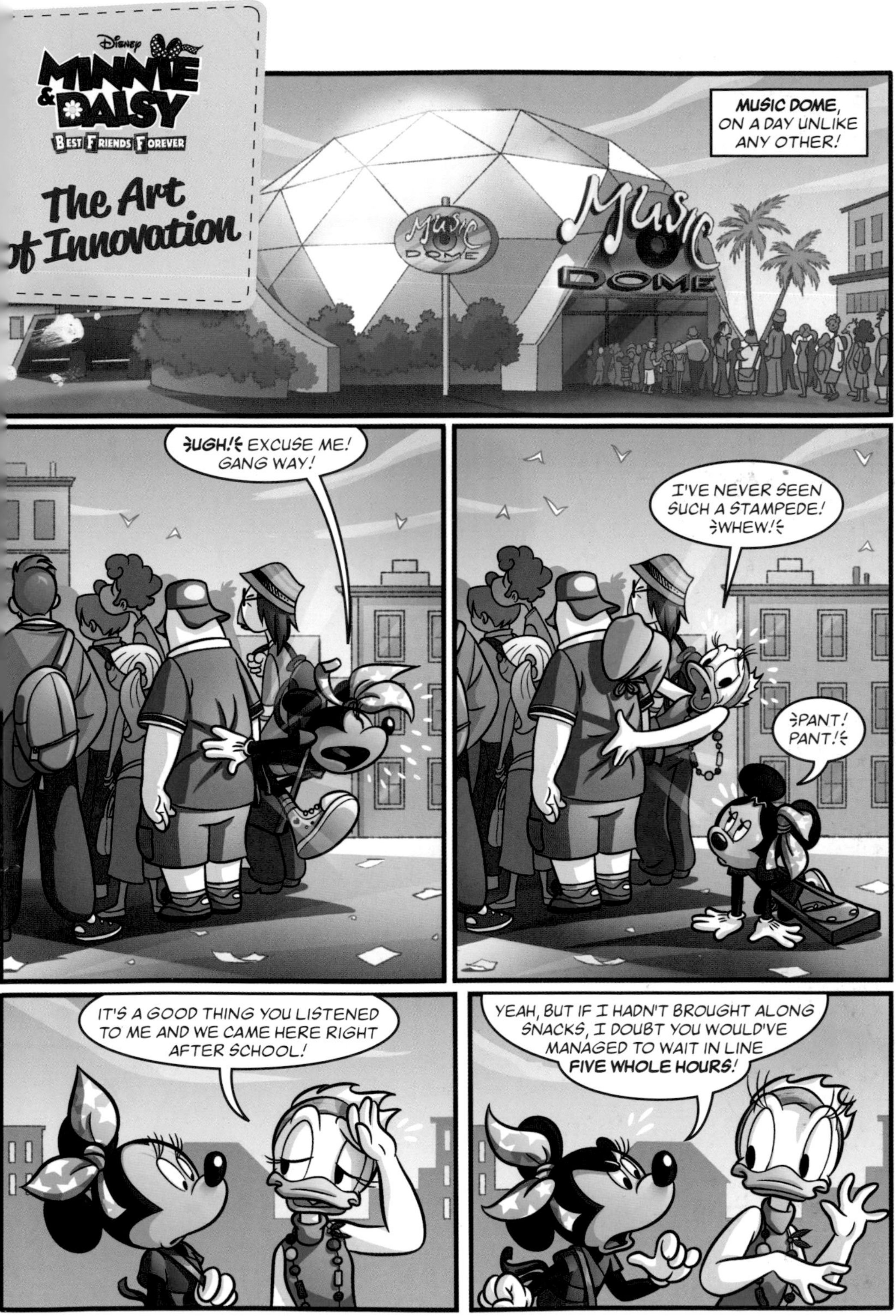
DISNEY
MINNIE & DAISY
BEST FRIENDS FOREVER
The Art of Innovation
MUSIC DOME, ON A DAY UNLIKE ANY OTHER!
MUSIC DOME
MUSIC DOME
UGH! EXCUSE ME! GANG WAY!
I'VE NEVER SEEN SUCH A STAMPEDE! WHEW!
PANT! PANT!
IT'S A GOOD THING YOU LISTENED TO ME AND WE CAME HERE RIGHT AFTER SCHOOL!
YEAH, BUT IF I HADN'T BROUGHT ALONG SNACKS, I DOUBT YOU WOULD'VE MANAGED TO WAIT IN LINE FIVE WHOLE HOURS!

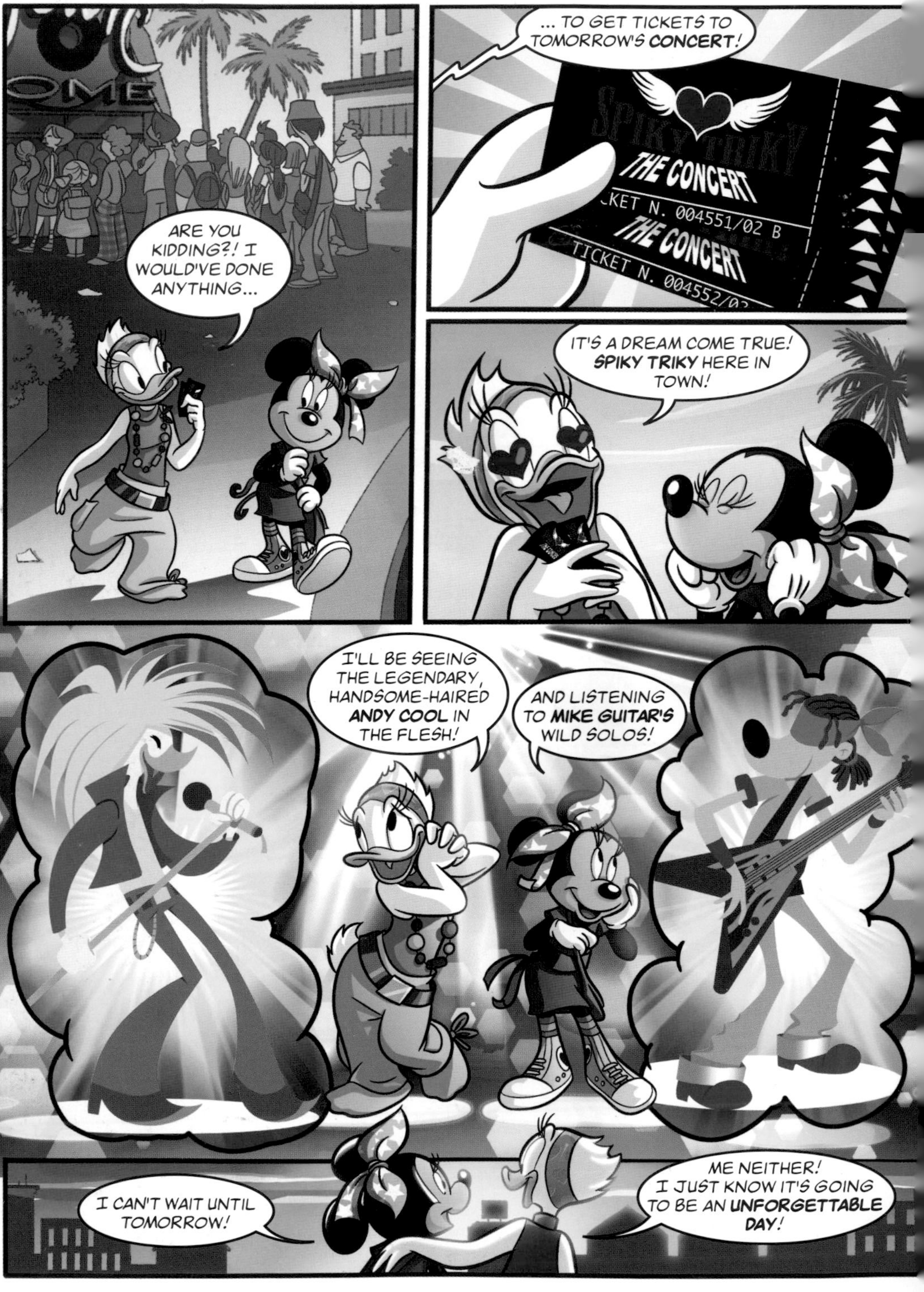
ARE YOU KIDDING?! I WOULD'VE DONE ANYTHING...
... TO GET TICKETS TO TOMORROW'S **CONCERT**!
SPIKY TRIKY
THE CONCERT
TICKET N. 004551/02 B
THE CONCERT
TICKET N. 004552/02
IT'S A DREAM COME TRUE! **SPIKY TRIKY** HERE IN TOWN!
I'LL BE SEEING THE LEGENDARY, HANDSOME-HAIRED **ANDY COOL** IN THE FLESH!
AND LISTENING TO **MIKE GUITAR'S** WILD SOLOS!
I CAN'T WAIT UNTIL TOMORROW!
ME NEITHER! I JUST KNOW IT'S GOING TO BE AN **UNFORGETTABLE DAY**!

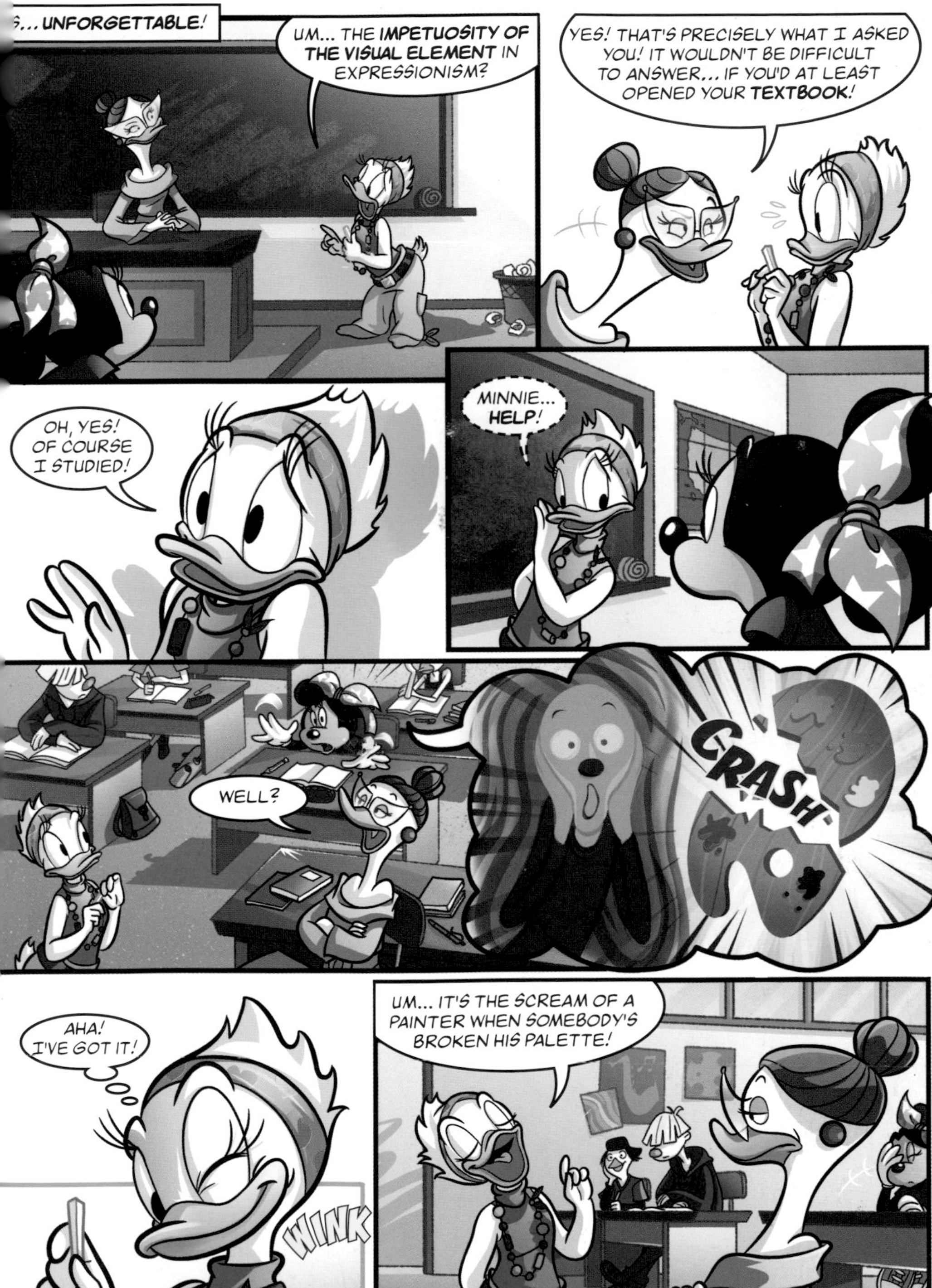
...UNFORGETTABLE!
UM... THE IMPETUOSITY OF THE VISUAL ELEMENT IN EXPRESSIONISM?
YES! THAT'S PRECISELY WHAT I ASKED YOU! IT WOULDN'T BE DIFFICULT TO ANSWER... IF YOU'D AT LEAST OPENED YOUR TEXTBOOK!
OH, YES! OF COURSE I STUDIED!
MINNIE... HELP!
WELL?
CRASH
AHA! I'VE GOT IT!
WINK
UM... IT'S THE SCREAM OF A PAINTER WHEN SOMEBODY'S BROKEN HIS PALETTE!

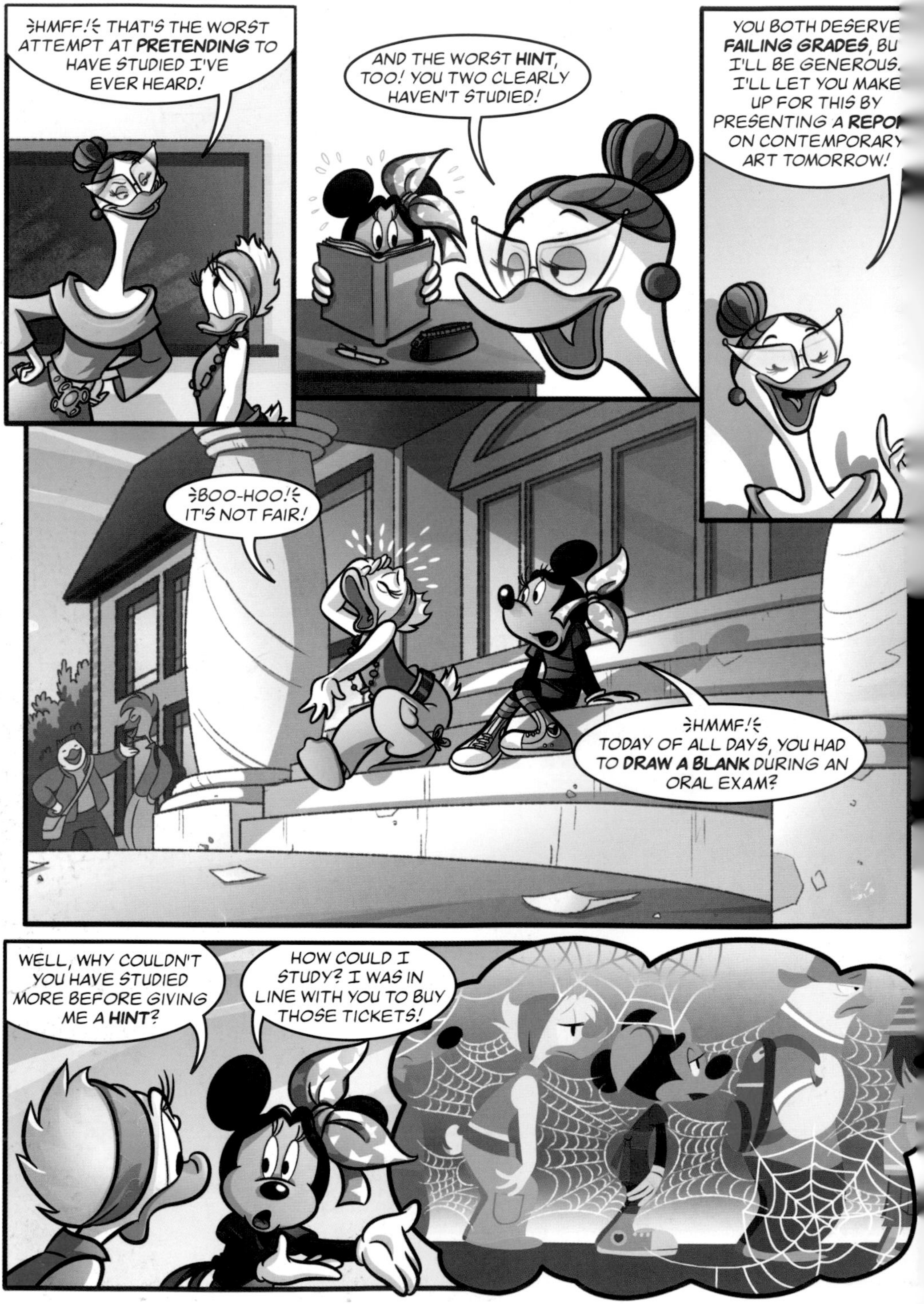

HMFF! THAT'S THE WORST ATTEMPT AT PRETENDING TO HAVE STUDIED I'VE EVER HEARD!
AND THE WORST HINT, TOO! YOU TWO CLEARLY HAVEN'T STUDIED!
YOU BOTH DESERVE FAILING GRADES, BU I'LL BE GENEROUS. I'LL LET YOU MAKE UP FOR THIS BY PRESENTING A REPO ON CONTEMPORARY ART TOMORROW!
BOO-HOO! IT'S NOT FAIR!
HMMF! TODAY OF ALL DAYS, YOU HAD TO DRAW A BLANK DURING AN ORAL EXAM?
WELL, WHY COULDN'T YOU HAVE STUDIED MORE BEFORE GIVING ME A HINT?
HOW COULD I STUDY? I WAS IN LINE WITH YOU TO BUY THOSE TICKETS!

HOW DEPRESSING! WE'LL BE SPENDING THE AFTERNOON IN THE LIBRARY INSTEAD OF AT THE BIGGEST EVENT OF THE YEAR!

≥SIGH!≤ MIKE GUITAR AND ANDY COOL WOULD NEVER GIVE UP ON THEIR DREAMS!

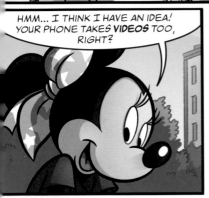

HMM... I THINK I HAVE AN IDEA! YOUR PHONE TAKES **VIDEOS** TOO, RIGHT?

AND SO...

DID YOU PUT YOUR PHONE IN **VIDEO MODE**?

YES! IT'S READY TO RECORD SOUND, TOO!

OUR FRIENDSHIP IS STRONGER THAN ANY TROUBLE!

PERFECT! LET'S GO, THEN!

I'LL ALWAYS BE WITH YOU!

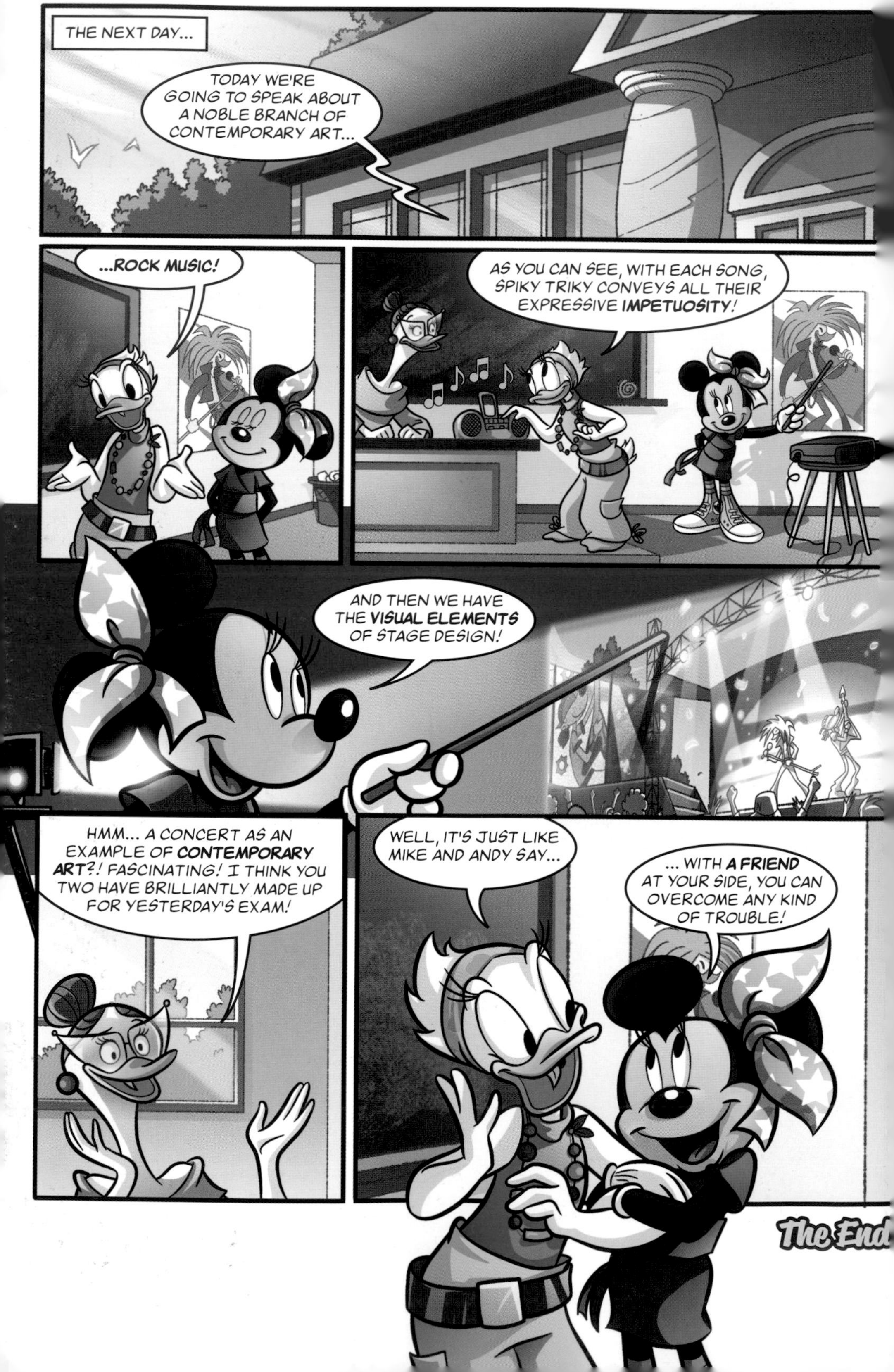
THE NEXT DAY...
TODAY WE'RE GOING TO SPEAK ABOUT A NOBLE BRANCH OF CONTEMPORARY ART...
...ROCK MUSIC!
AS YOU CAN SEE, WITH EACH SONG, SPIKY TRIKY CONVEYS ALL THEIR EXPRESSIVE IMPETUOSITY!
AND THEN WE HAVE THE VISUAL ELEMENTS OF STAGE DESIGN!
HMM... A CONCERT AS AN EXAMPLE OF CONTEMPORARY ART?! FASCINATING! I THINK YOU TWO HAVE BRILLIANTLY MADE UP FOR YESTERDAY'S EXAM!
WELL, IT'S JUST LIKE MIKE AND ANDY SAY...
... WITH A FRIEND AT YOUR SIDE, YOU CAN OVERCOME ANY KIND OF TROUBLE!
The End

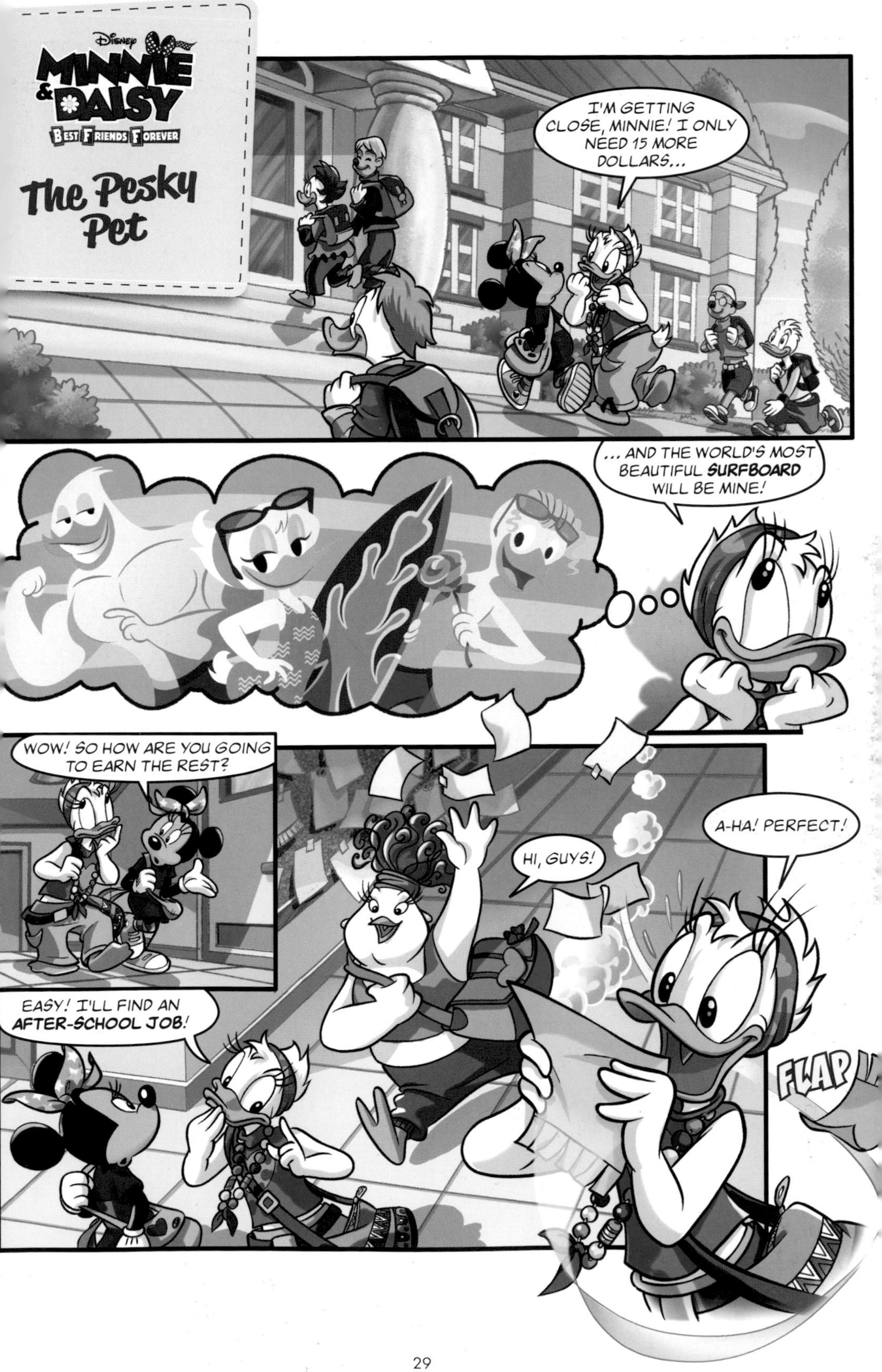
Disney
MINNIE & DAISY
BEST FRIENDS FOREVER
The Pesky Pet
I'M GETTING CLOSE, MINNIE! I ONLY NEED 15 MORE DOLLARS...
... AND THE WORLD'S MOST BEAUTIFUL SURFBOARD WILL BE MINE!
WOW! SO HOW ARE YOU GOING TO EARN THE REST?
EASY! I'LL FIND AN AFTER-SCHOOL JOB!
HI, GUYS!
A-HA! PERFECT!
FLAP

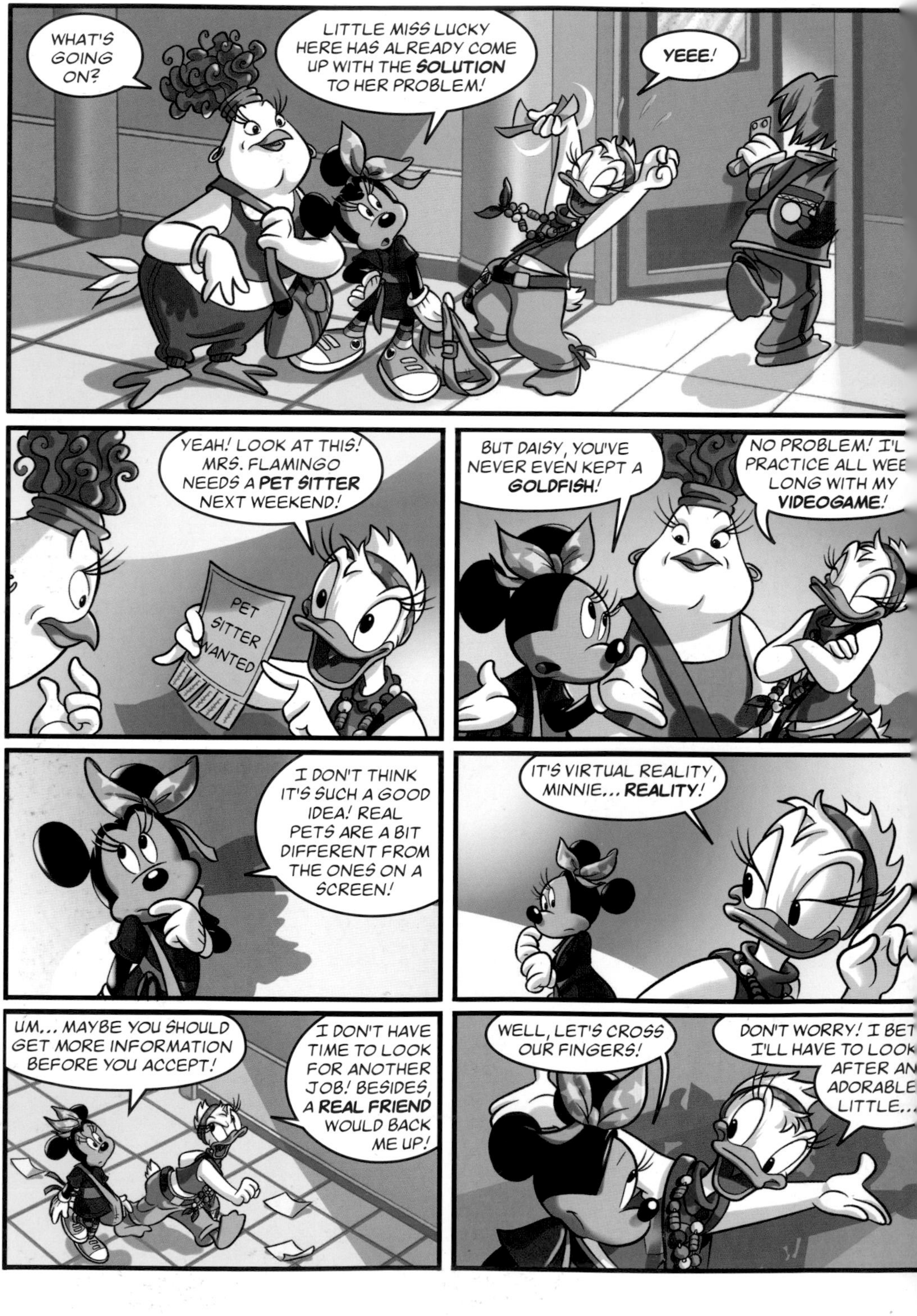
WHAT'S GOING ON?
LITTLE MISS LUCKY HERE HAS ALREADY COME UP WITH THE SOLUTION TO HER PROBLEM!
YEEE!
YEAH! LOOK AT THIS! MRS. FLAMINGO NEEDS A PET SITTER NEXT WEEKEND!
PET SITTER WANTED
BUT DAISY, YOU'VE NEVER EVEN KEPT A GOLDFISH!
NO PROBLEM! I'L PRACTICE ALL WEE LONG WITH MY VIDEOGAME!
I DON'T THINK IT'S SUCH A GOOD IDEA! REAL PETS ARE A BIT DIFFERENT FROM THE ONES ON A SCREEN!
IT'S VIRTUAL REALITY, MINNIE... REALITY!
UM... MAYBE YOU SHOULD GET MORE INFORMATION BEFORE YOU ACCEPT!
I DON'T HAVE TIME TO LOOK FOR ANOTHER JOB! BESIDES, A REAL FRIEND WOULD BACK ME UP!
WELL, LET'S CROSS OUR FINGERS!
DON'T WORRY! I BET I'LL HAVE TO LOOK AFTER AN ADORABLE LITTLE...

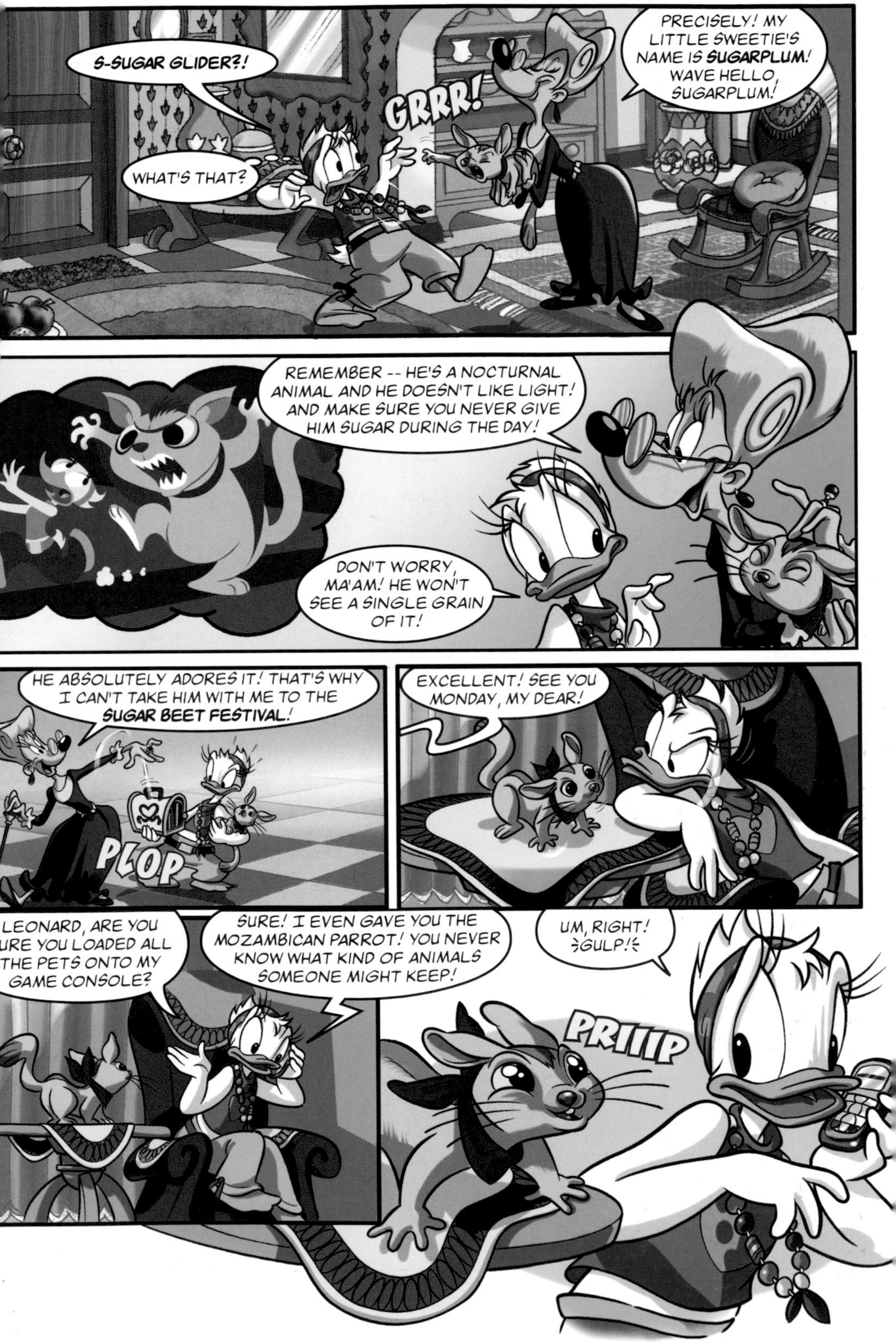
S-SUGAR GLIDER?!
WHAT'S THAT?
GRRR!
PRECISELY! MY LITTLE SWEETIE'S NAME IS SUGARPLUM! WAVE HELLO, SUGARPLUM!
REMEMBER -- HE'S A NOCTURNAL ANIMAL AND HE DOESN'T LIKE LIGHT! AND MAKE SURE YOU NEVER GIVE HIM SUGAR DURING THE DAY!
DON'T WORRY, MA'AM! HE WON'T SEE A SINGLE GRAIN OF IT!
HE ABSOLUTELY ADORES IT! THAT'S WHY I CAN'T TAKE HIM WITH ME TO THE SUGAR BEET FESTIVAL!
PLOP
EXCELLENT! SEE YOU MONDAY, MY DEAR!
LEONARD, ARE YOU SURE YOU LOADED ALL THE PETS ONTO MY GAME CONSOLE?
SURE! I EVEN GAVE YOU THE MOZAMBICAN PARROT! YOU NEVER KNOW WHAT KIND OF ANIMALS SOMEONE MIGHT KEEP!
UM, RIGHT! GULP!
PRIIIP

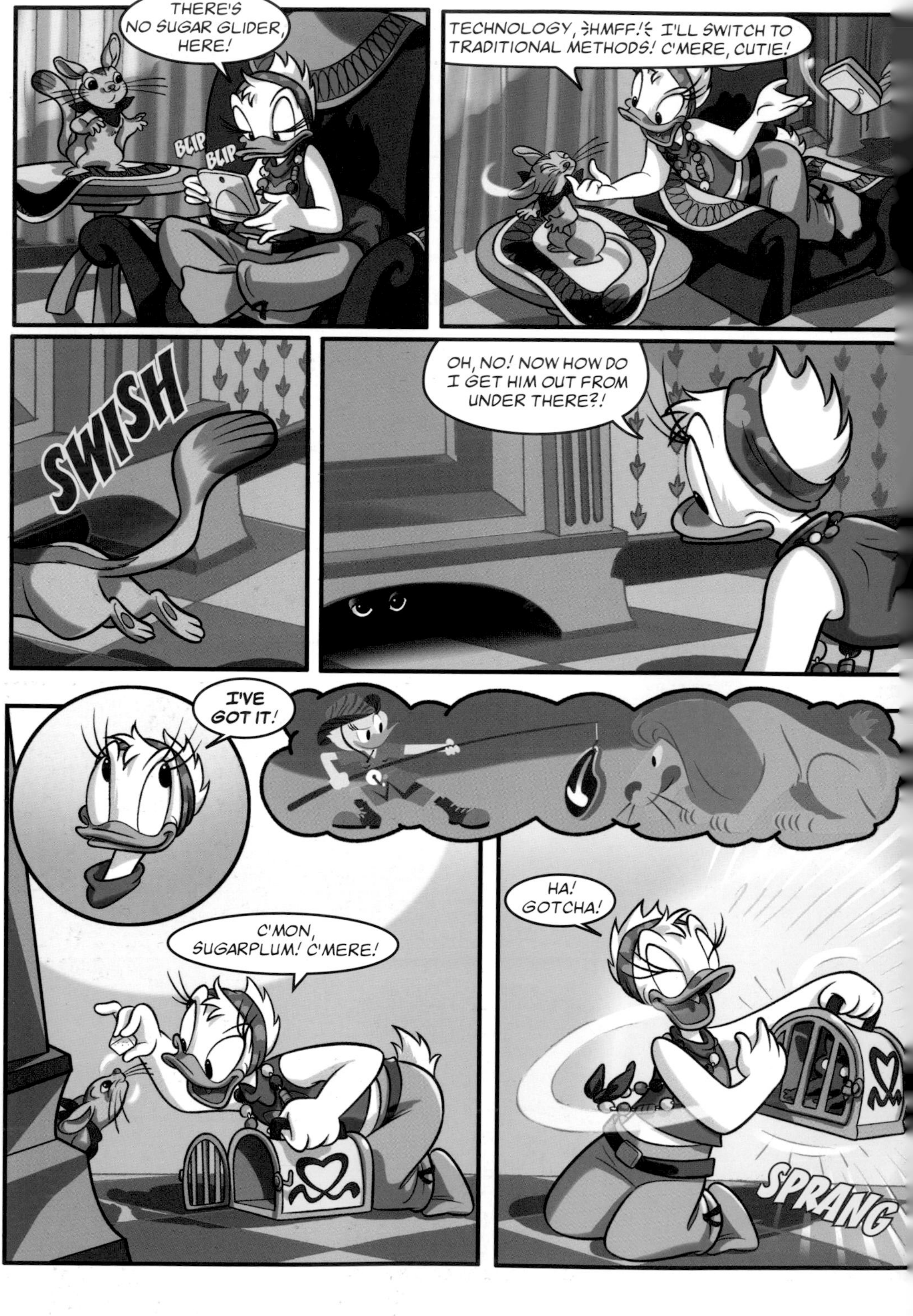
THERE'S NO SUGAR GLIDER, HERE!
BLIP BLIP
TECHNOLOGY, HMFF! I'LL SWITCH TO TRADITIONAL METHODS! C'MERE, CUTIE!
SWISH
OH, NO! NOW HOW DO I GET HIM OUT FROM UNDER THERE?!
I'VE GOT IT!
C'MON, SUGARPLUM! C'MERE!
HA! GOTCHA!
SPRANG

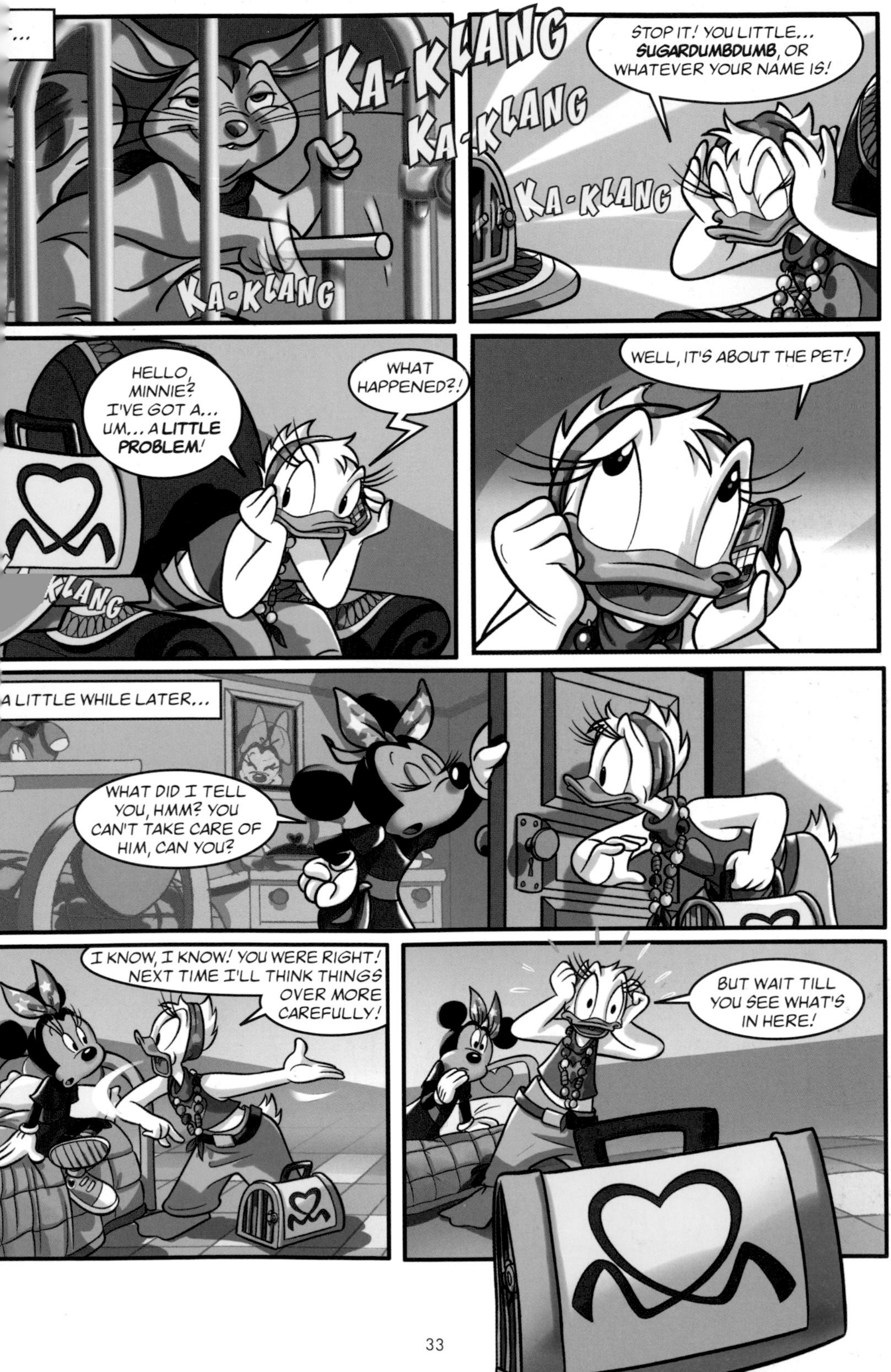
...
KA-KLANG
KA-KLANG
KA-KLANG
KA-KLANG
STOP IT! YOU LITTLE... **SUGARDUMBDUMB**, OR WHATEVER YOUR NAME IS!
HELLO, MINNIE? I'VE GOT A... UM... A **LITTLE PROBLEM**!
WHAT HAPPENED?!
KLANG
WELL, IT'S ABOUT THE PET!
A LITTLE WHILE LATER...
WHAT DID I TELL YOU, HMM? YOU CAN'T TAKE CARE OF HIM, CAN YOU?
I KNOW, I KNOW! YOU WERE RIGHT! NEXT TIME I'LL THINK THINGS OVER MORE CAREFULLY!
BUT WAIT TILL YOU SEE WHAT'S IN HERE!

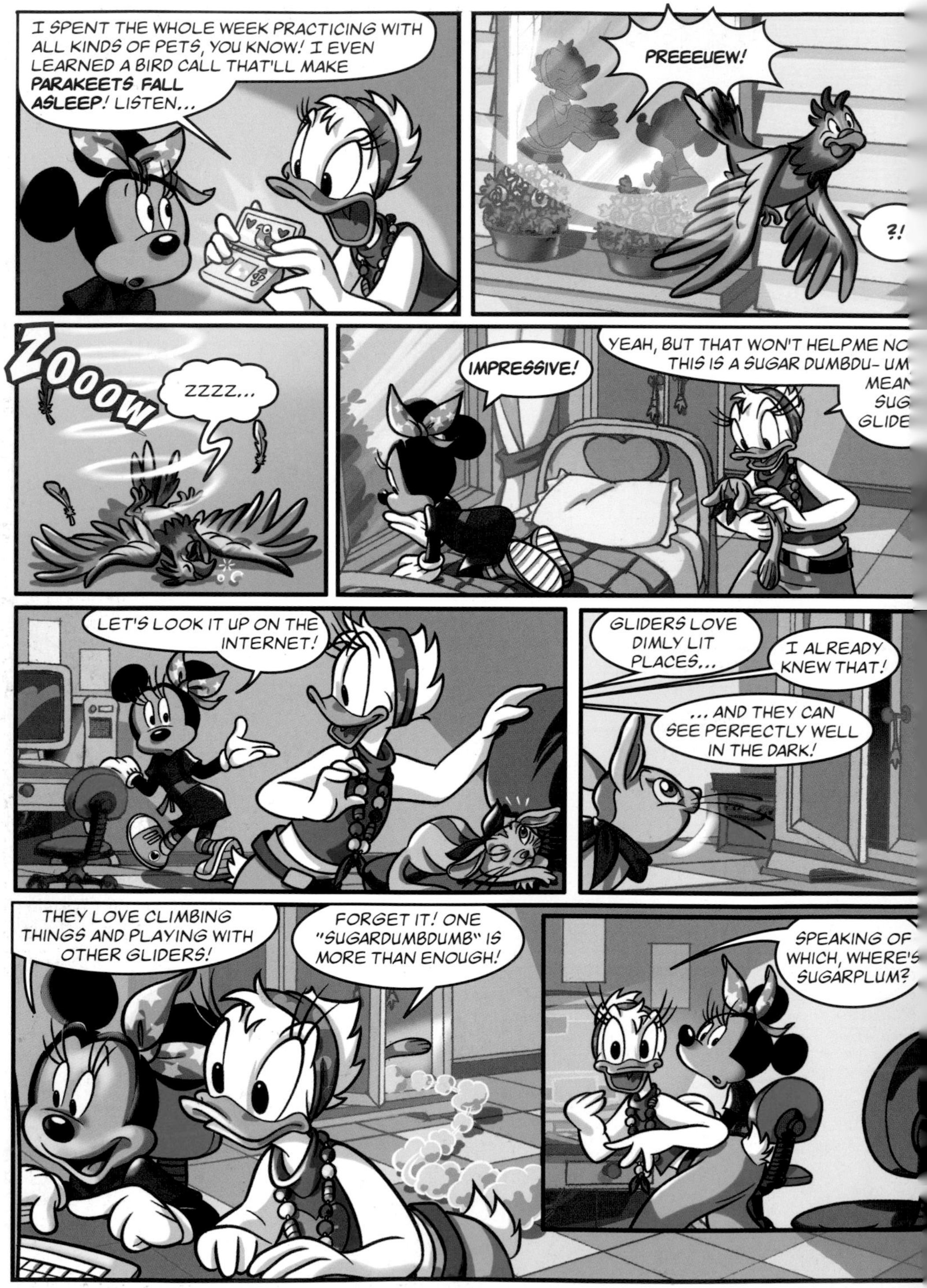
I SPENT THE WHOLE WEEK PRACTICING WITH ALL KINDS OF PETS, YOU KNOW! I EVEN LEARNED A BIRD CALL THAT'LL MAKE **PARAKEETS FALL ASLEEP**! LISTEN...
PREEEUEW!
?!
ZOOOW
ZZZZ...
IMPRESSIVE!
YEAH, BUT THAT WON'T HELPME NO
THIS IS A SUGAR DUMBDU- UM,
MEAN
SUG
GLIDE
LET'S LOOK IT UP ON THE INTERNET!
GLIDERS LOVE DIMLY LIT PLACES...
I ALREADY KNEW THAT!
... AND THEY CAN SEE PERFECTLY WELL IN THE DARK!
THEY LOVE CLIMBING THINGS AND PLAYING WITH OTHER GLIDERS!
FORGET IT! ONE "SUGARDUMBDUMB" IS MORE THAN ENOUGH!
SPEAKING OF WHICH, WHERE'S SUGARPLUM?

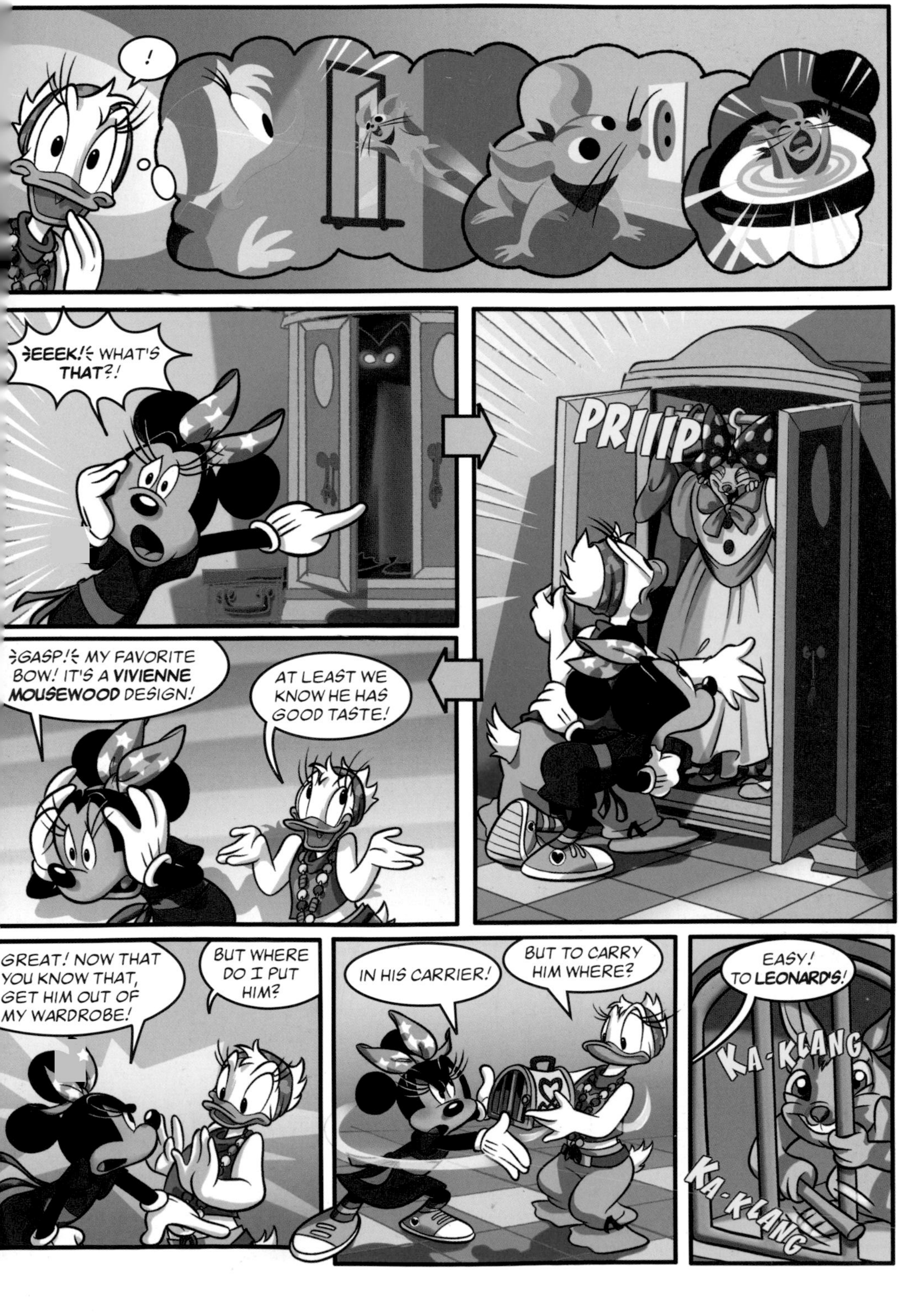
!
≷EEEK!≶ WHAT'S THAT?!
PRIIIP
≷GASP!≶ MY FAVORITE BOW! IT'S A **VIVIENNE MOUSEWOOD** DESIGN!
AT LEAST WE KNOW HE HAS GOOD TASTE!
GREAT! NOW THAT YOU KNOW THAT, GET HIM OUT OF MY WARDROBE!
BUT WHERE DO I PUT HIM?
IN HIS CARRIER!
BUT TO CARRY HIM WHERE?
EASY! TO **LEONARD'S**!
KA-KLANG
KA-KLANG

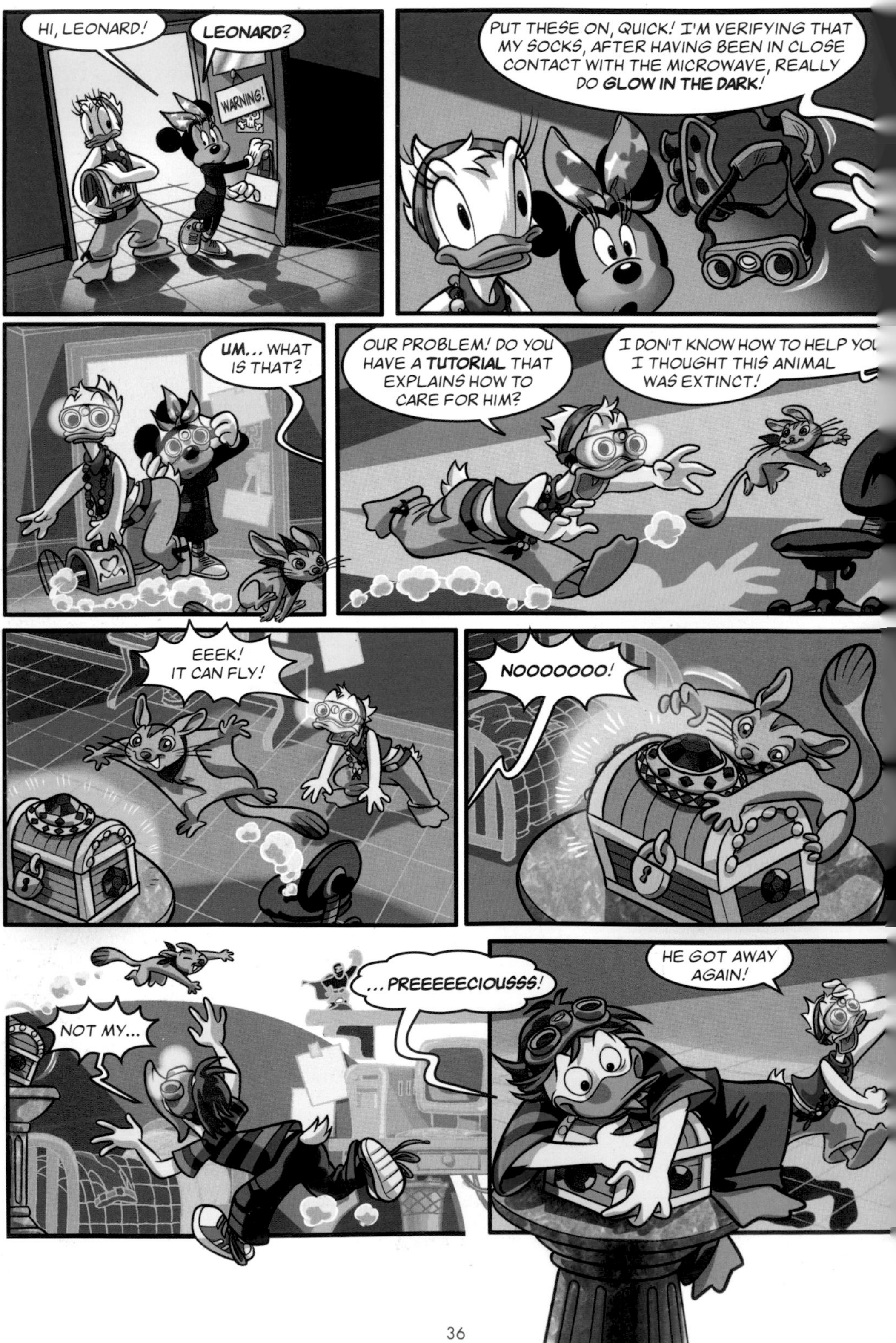
HI, LEONARD!
LEONARD?
WARNING!
PUT THESE ON, QUICK! I'M VERIFYING THAT MY SOCKS, AFTER HAVING BEEN IN CLOSE CONTACT WITH THE MICROWAVE, REALLY DO GLOW IN THE DARK!
UM... WHAT IS THAT?
OUR PROBLEM! DO YOU HAVE A TUTORIAL THAT EXPLAINS HOW TO CARE FOR HIM?
I DON'T KNOW HOW TO HELP YOU I THOUGHT THIS ANIMAL WAS EXTINCT!
EEEK! IT CAN FLY!
NOOOOOOO!
NOT MY...
...PREEEEECIOUSSS!
HE GOT AWAY AGAIN!

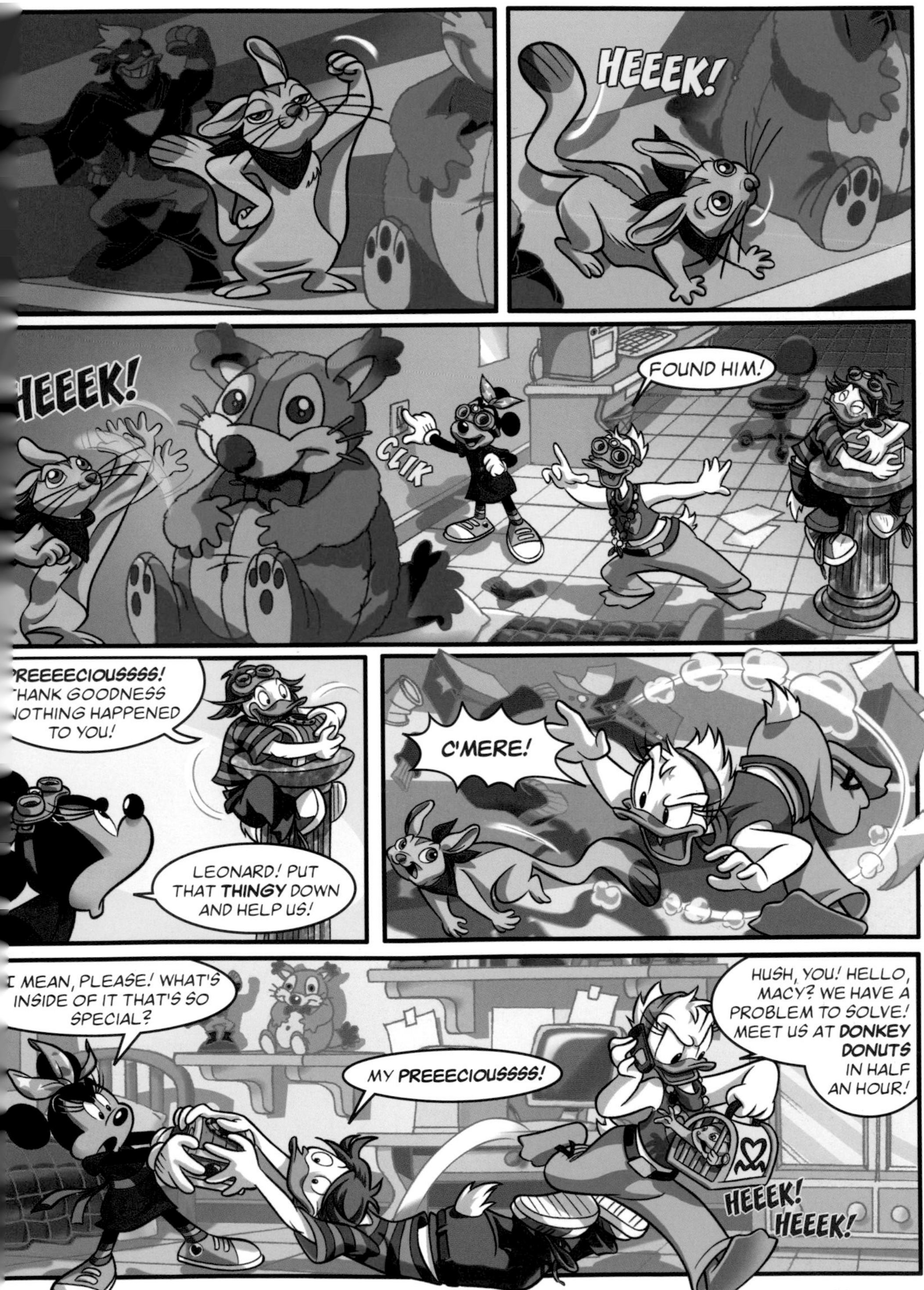
HEEEK!
HEEEK!
FOUND HIM!
CLIK
PREEEECIOUSSSS! THANK GOODNESS NOTHING HAPPENED TO YOU!
LEONARD! PUT THAT THINGY DOWN AND HELP US!
C'MERE!
I MEAN, PLEASE! WHAT'S INSIDE OF IT THAT'S SO SPECIAL?
MY PREEECIOUSSSS!
HUSH, YOU! HELLO, MACY? WE HAVE A PROBLEM TO SOLVE! MEET US AT DONKEY DONUTS IN HALF AN HOUR!
HEEEK! HEEEK!

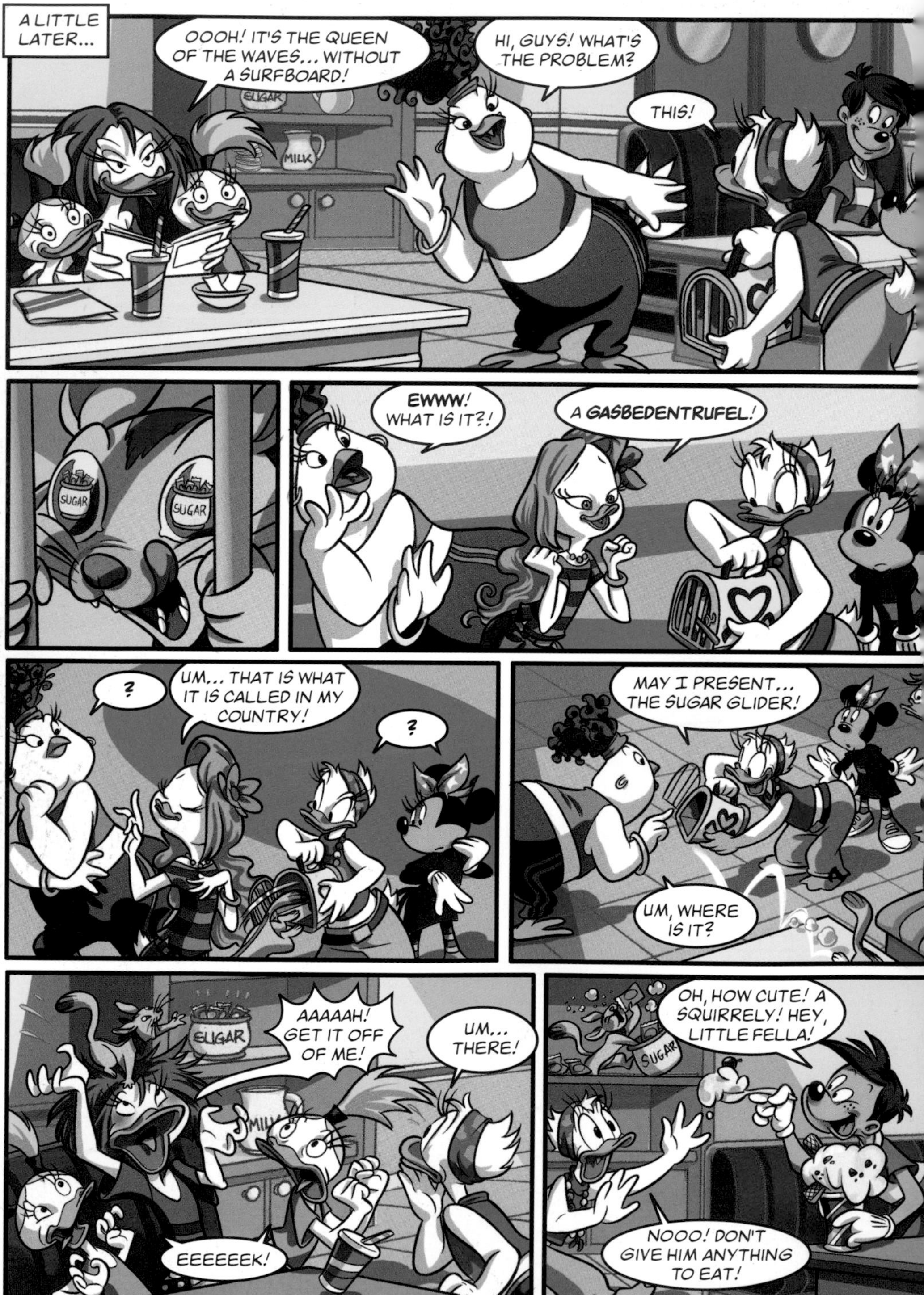
A LITTLE LATER...
OOOH! IT'S THE QUEEN OF THE WAVES... WITHOUT A SURFBOARD!
SUGAR
MILK
HI, GUYS! WHAT'S THE PROBLEM?
THIS!
SUGAR
SUGAR
EWWW! WHAT IS IT?!
A GASBEDENTRUFEL!
?
UM... THAT IS WHAT IT IS CALLED IN MY COUNTRY!
?
MAY I PRESENT... THE SUGAR GLIDER!
UM, WHERE IS IT?
SUGAR
AAAAAH! GET IT OFF OF ME!
UM... THERE!
MILK
EEEEEEK!
OH, HOW CUTE! A SQUIRRELY! HEY, LITTLE FELLA!
SUGAR
NOOO! DON'T GIVE HIM ANYTHING TO EAT!

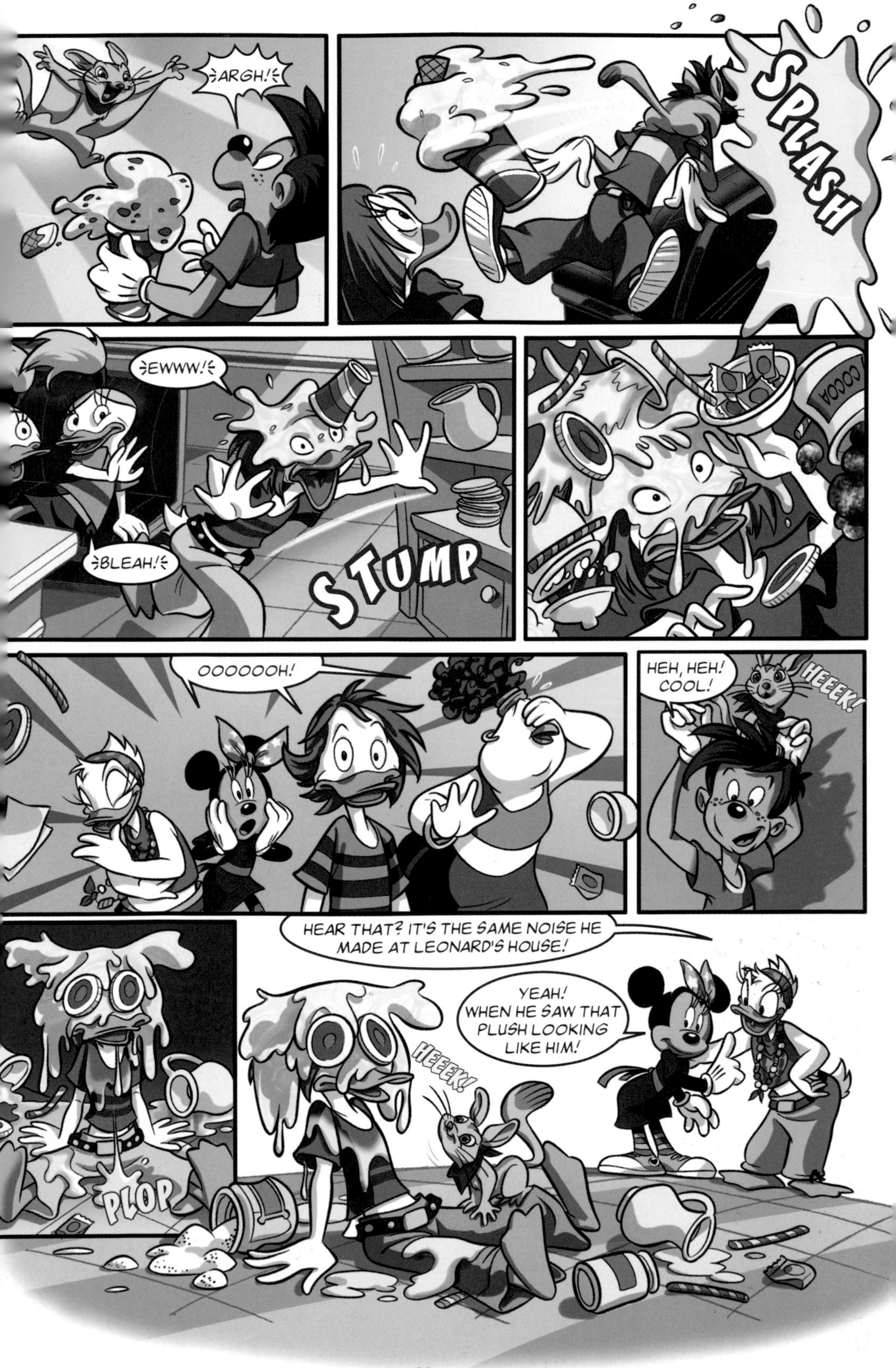
ARGH!
SPLASH
EWWW!
BLEAH!
STUMP
OOOOOOH!
HEH, HEH! COOL!
HEEEK!
HEAR THAT? IT'S THE SAME NOISE HE MADE AT LEONARD'S HOUSE!
YEAH! WHEN HE SAW THAT PLUSH LOOKING LIKE HIM!
PLOP
HEEEK!

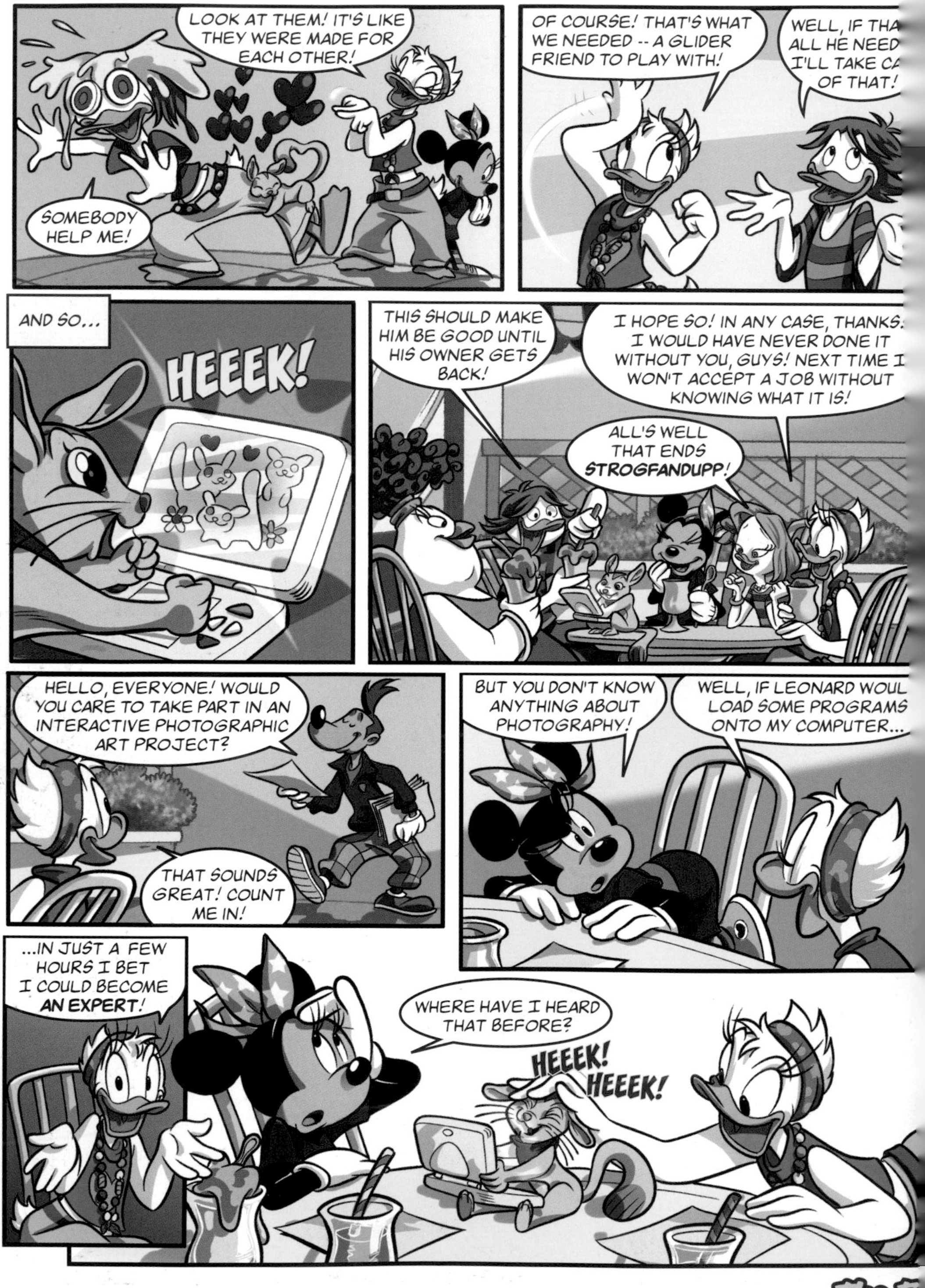
LOOK AT THEM! IT'S LIKE THEY WERE MADE FOR EACH OTHER!
SOMEBODY HELP ME!
OF COURSE! THAT'S WHAT WE NEEDED -- A GLIDER FRIEND TO PLAY WITH!
WELL, IF THA ALL HE NEED I'LL TAKE CA OF THAT!
AND SO...
HEEEK!
THIS SHOULD MAKE HIM BE GOOD UNTIL HIS OWNER GETS BACK!
I HOPE SO! IN ANY CASE, THANKS! I WOULD HAVE NEVER DONE IT WITHOUT YOU, GUYS! NEXT TIME I WON'T ACCEPT A JOB WITHOUT KNOWING WHAT IT IS!
ALL'S WELL THAT ENDS STROGFANDUPP!
HELLO, EVERYONE! WOULD YOU CARE TO TAKE PART IN AN INTERACTIVE PHOTOGRAPHIC ART PROJECT?
THAT SOUNDS GREAT! COUNT ME IN!
BUT YOU DON'T KNOW ANYTHING ABOUT PHOTOGRAPHY!
WELL, IF LEONARD WOUL LOAD SOME PROGRAMS ONTO MY COMPUTER...
...IN JUST A FEW HOURS I BET I COULD BECOME AN EXPERT!
WHERE HAVE I HEARD THAT BEFORE?
HEEEK! HEEEK!
The E

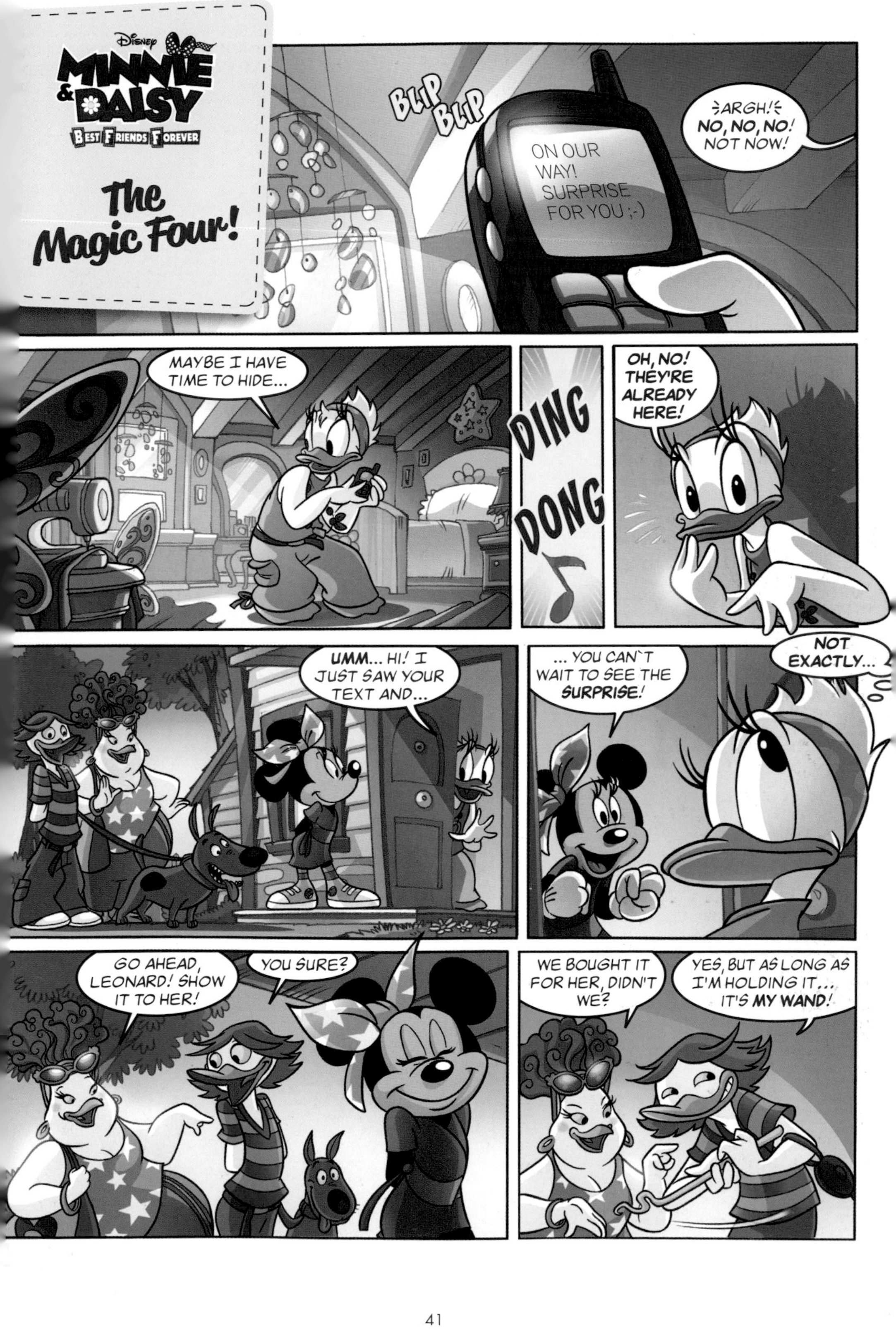
Disney
MINNIE & DAISY
BEST FRIENDS FOREVER
The Magic Four!
BLIP BLIP
ON OUR WAY! SURPRISE FOR YOU ;-)
ARGH! NO, NO, NO! NOT NOW!
MAYBE I HAVE TIME TO HIDE...
DING DONG
OH, NO! THEY'RE ALREADY HERE!
UMM... HI! I JUST SAW YOUR TEXT AND...
... YOU CAN'T WAIT TO SEE THE SURPRISE!
NOT EXACTLY...
GO AHEAD, LEONARD! SHOW IT TO HER!
YOU SURE?
WE BOUGHT IT FOR HER, DIDN'T WE?
YES, BUT AS LONG AS I'M HOLDING IT... IT'S MY WAND!

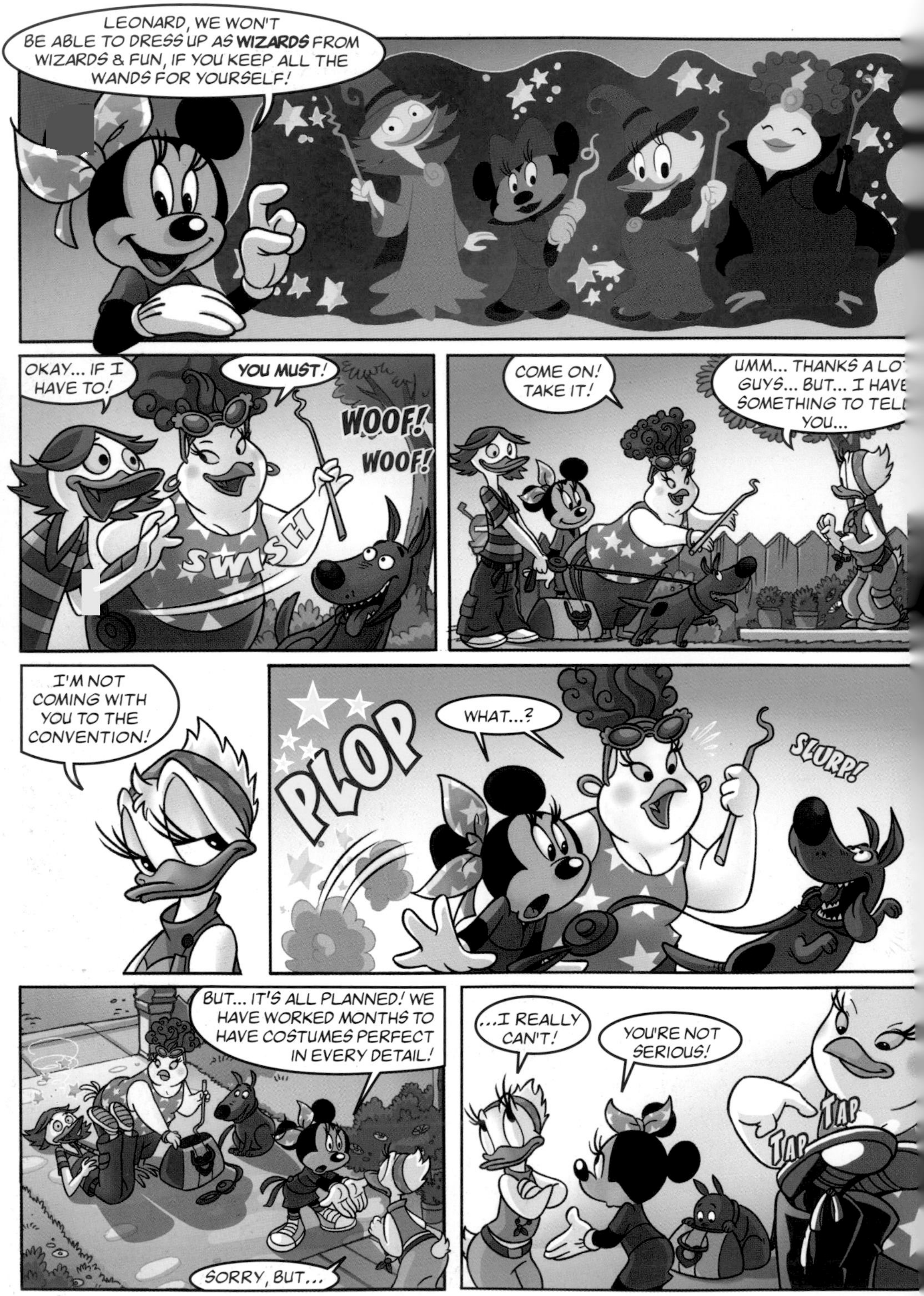
LEONARD, WE WON'T BE ABLE TO DRESS UP AS WIZARDS FROM WIZARDS & FUN, IF YOU KEEP ALL THE WANDS FOR YOURSELF!
OKAY... IF I HAVE TO!
YOU MUST!
WOOF!
WOOF!
SWISH
COME ON! TAKE IT!
UMM... THANKS A LOT GUYS... BUT... I HAVE SOMETHING TO TELL YOU...
I'M NOT COMING WITH YOU TO THE CONVENTION!
PLOP
WHAT...?
SLURP!
BUT... IT'S ALL PLANNED! WE HAVE WORKED MONTHS TO HAVE COSTUMES PERFECT IN EVERY DETAIL!
SORRY, BUT...
...I REALLY CAN'T!
YOU'RE NOT SERIOUS!
TAP
TAP

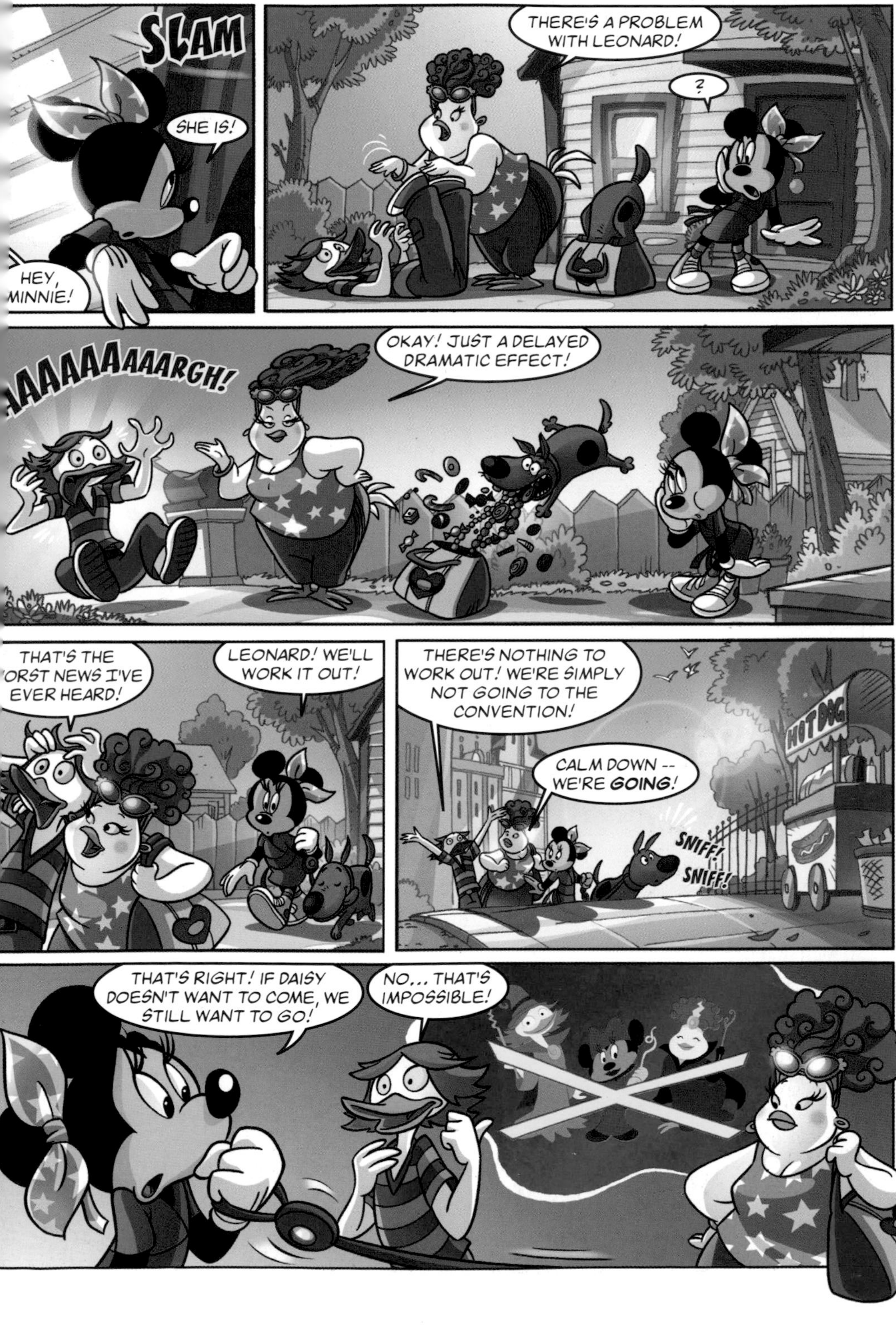
SLAM
SHE IS!
HEY, MINNIE!
THERE'S A PROBLEM WITH LEONARD!
?
AAAAAAAAARGH!
OKAY! JUST A DELAYED DRAMATIC EFFECT!
THAT'S THE ORST NEWS I'VE EVER HEARD!
LEONARD! WE'LL WORK IT OUT!
THERE'S NOTHING TO WORK OUT! WE'RE SIMPLY NOT GOING TO THE CONVENTION!
CALM DOWN -- WE'RE GOING!
HOT DOG
SNIFF! SNIFF!
THAT'S RIGHT! IF DAISY DOESN'T WANT TO COME, WE STILL WANT TO GO!
NO... THAT'S IMPOSSIBLE!

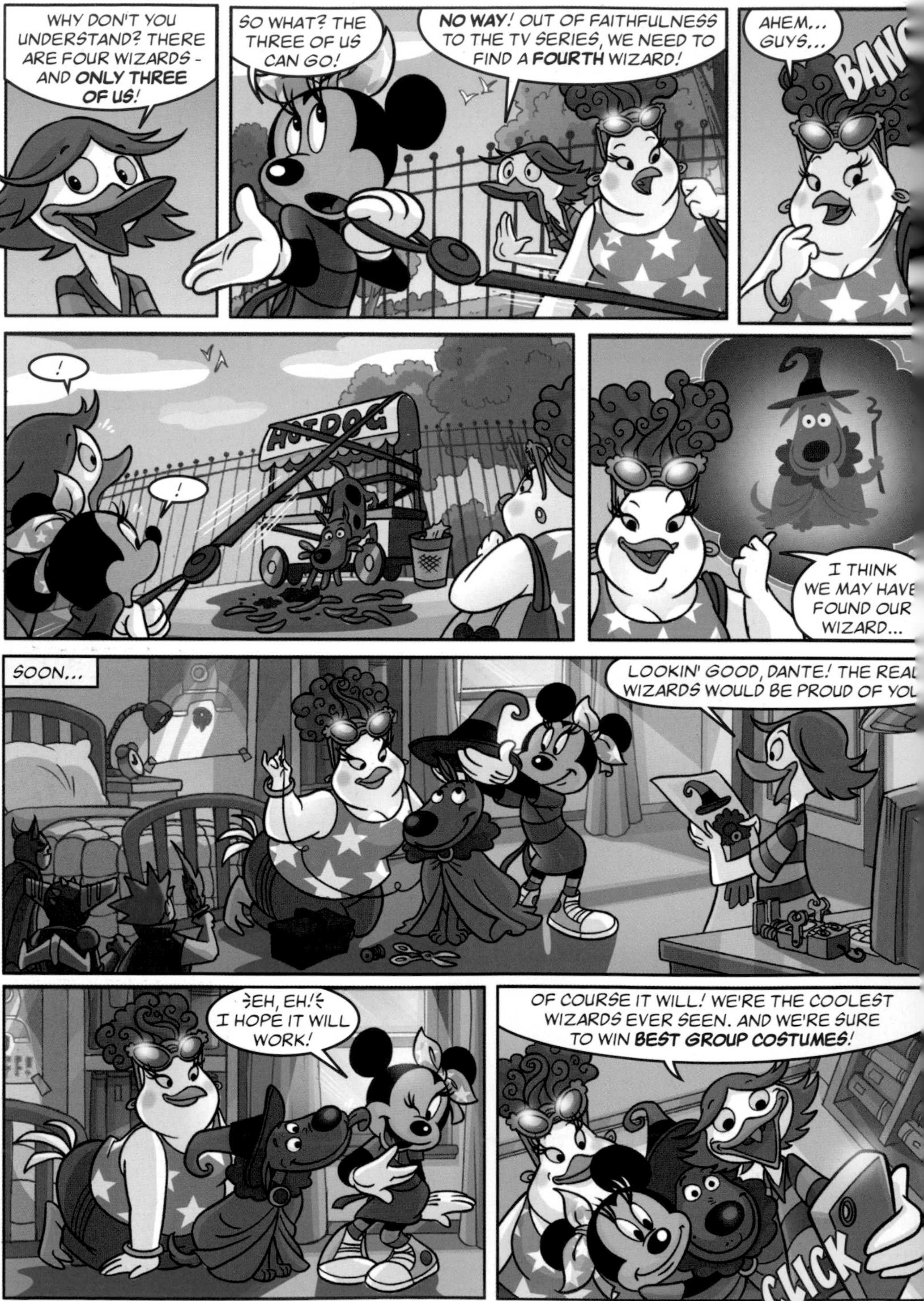
WHY DON'T YOU UNDERSTAND? THERE ARE FOUR WIZARDS - AND ONLY THREE OF US!
SO WHAT? THE THREE OF US CAN GO!
NO WAY! OUT OF FAITHFULNESS TO THE TV SERIES, WE NEED TO FIND A FOURTH WIZARD!
AHEM... GUYS...
!
!
HOT DOG
I THINK WE MAY HAVE FOUND OUR WIZARD...
SOON...
LOOKIN' GOOD, DANTE! THE REAL WIZARDS WOULD BE PROUD OF YOU
EH, EH! I HOPE IT WILL WORK!
OF COURSE IT WILL! WE'RE THE COOLEST WIZARDS EVER SEEN. AND WE'RE SURE TO WIN BEST GROUP COSTUMES!
CLICK

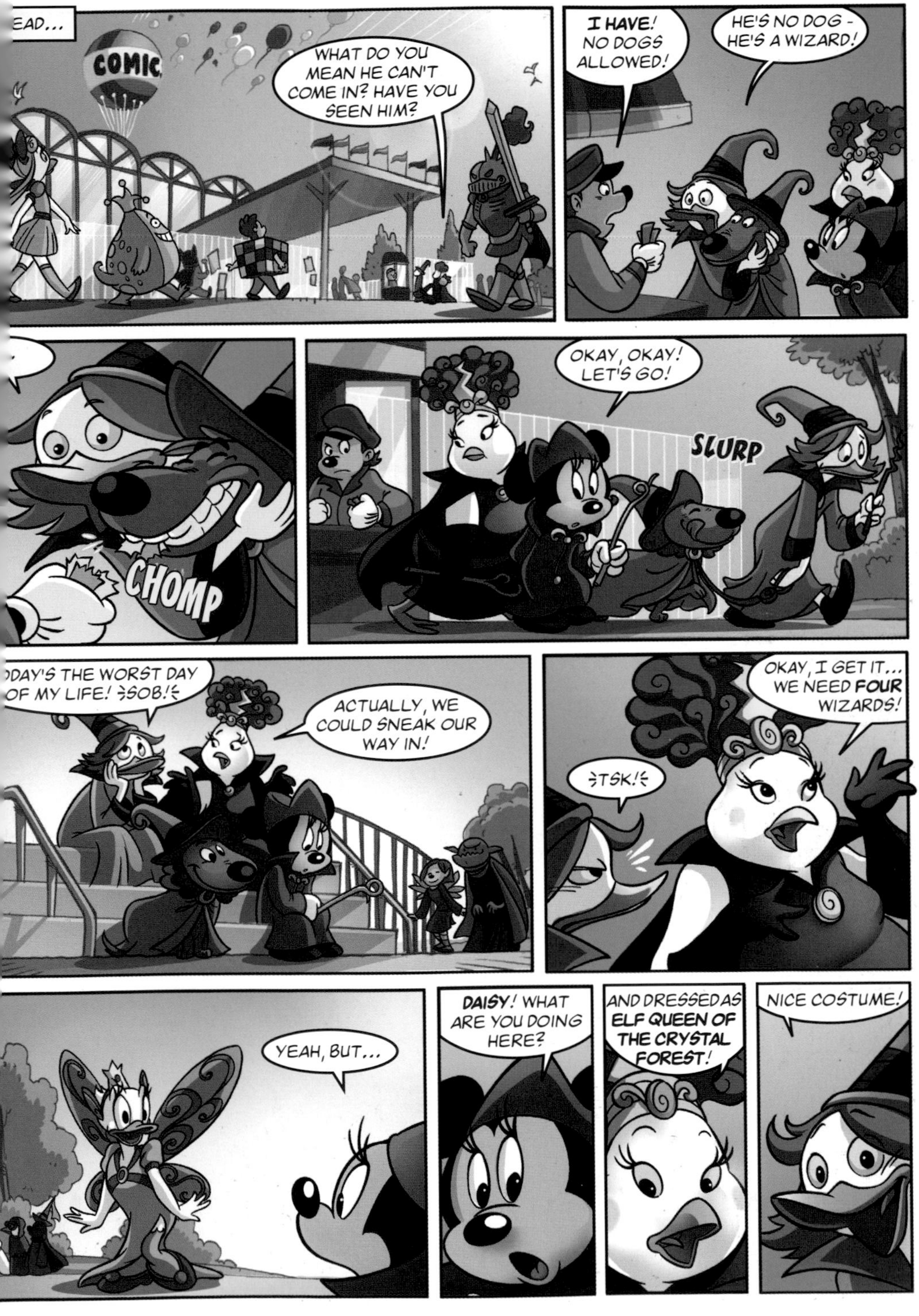
EAD...
COMIC
WHAT DO YOU MEAN HE CAN'T COME IN? HAVE YOU SEEN HIM?
I HAVE! NO DOGS ALLOWED!
HE'S NO DOG - HE'S A WIZARD!
CHOMP
OKAY, OKAY! LET'S GO!
SLURP
DAY'S THE WORST DAY OF MY LIFE! SOB!
ACTUALLY, WE COULD SNEAK OUR WAY IN!
OKAY, I GET IT... WE NEED FOUR WIZARDS!
TSK!
YEAH, BUT...
DAISY! WHAT ARE YOU DOING HERE?
AND DRESSED AS ELF QUEEN OF THE CRYSTAL FOREST!
NICE COSTUME!

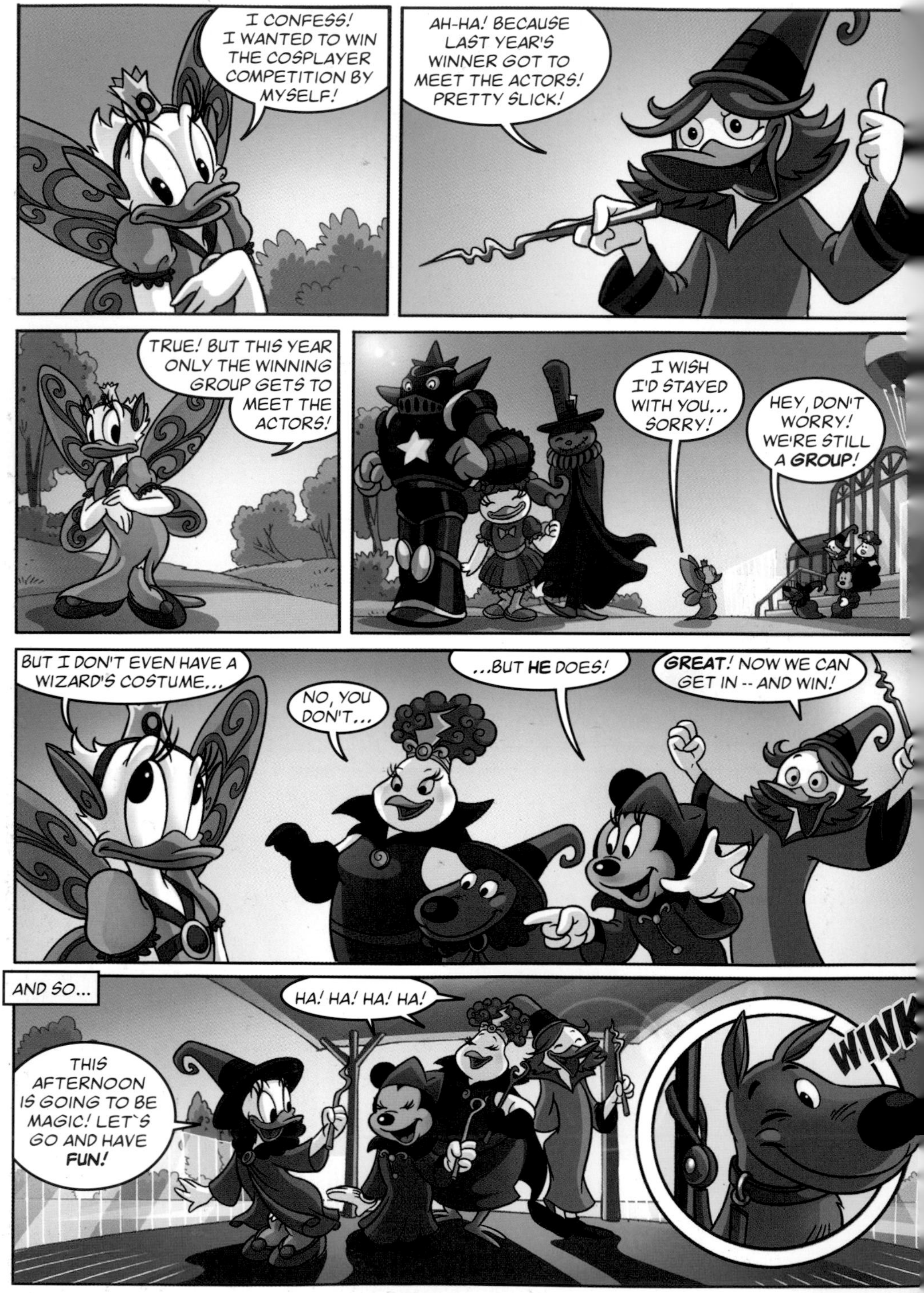
I CONFESS! I WANTED TO WIN THE COSPLAYER COMPETITION BY MYSELF!
AH-HA! BECAUSE LAST YEAR'S WINNER GOT TO MEET THE ACTORS! PRETTY SLICK!
TRUE! BUT THIS YEAR ONLY THE WINNING GROUP GETS TO MEET THE ACTORS!
I WISH I'D STAYED WITH YOU... SORRY!
HEY, DON'T WORRY! WE'RE STILL A **GROUP**!
BUT I DON'T EVEN HAVE A WIZARD'S COSTUME...
NO, YOU DON'T...
...BUT **HE** DOES!
GREAT! NOW WE CAN GET IN -- AND WIN!
AND SO...
HA! HA! HA! HA!
THIS AFTERNOON IS GOING TO BE MAGIC! LET'S GO AND HAVE **FUN**!
WINK
The End

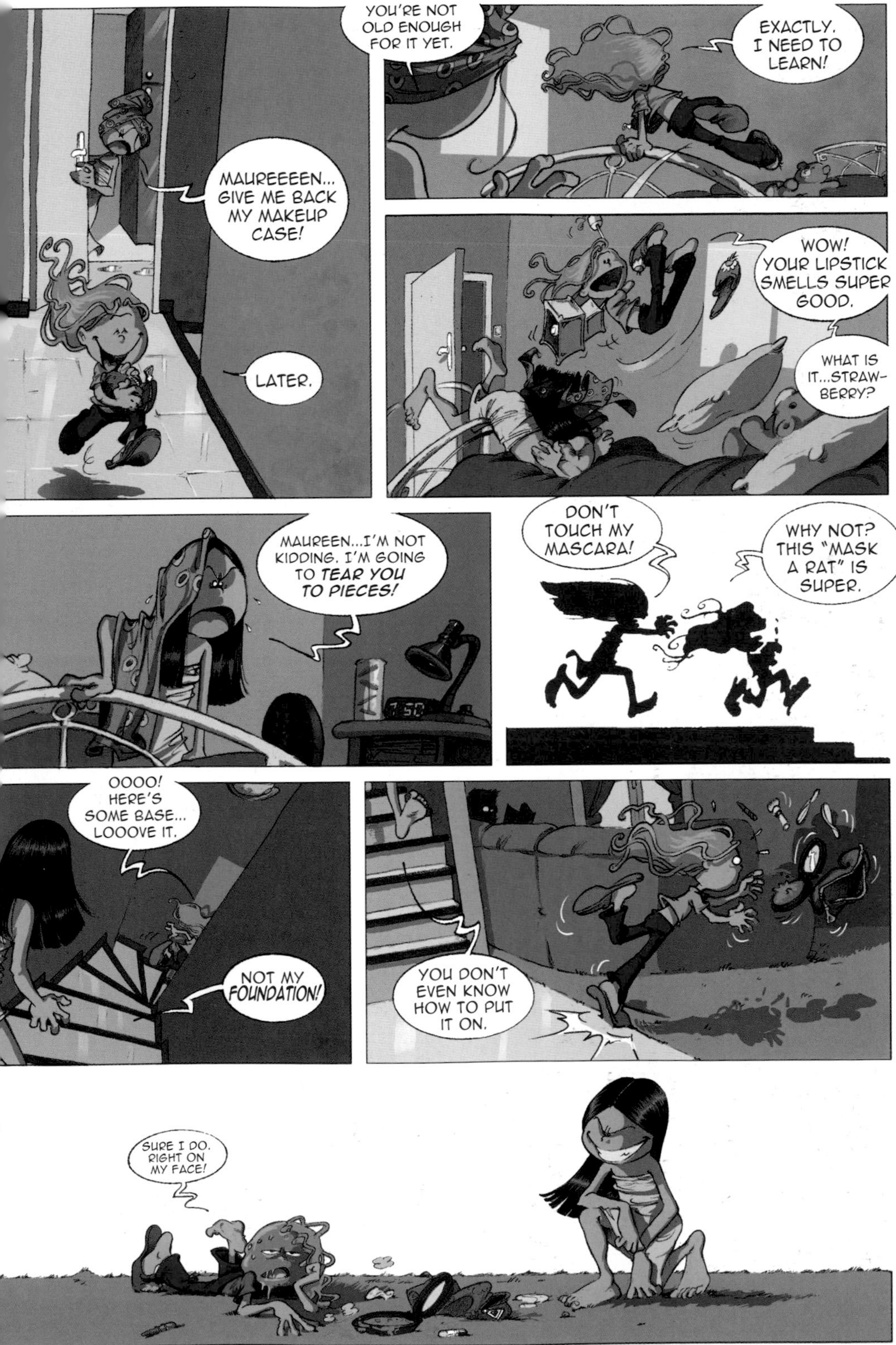
MAUREEEEN... GIVE ME BACK MY MAKEUP CASE!
LATER.
YOU'RE NOT OLD ENOUGH FOR IT YET.
EXACTLY. I NEED TO LEARN!
WOW! YOUR LIPSTICK SMELLS SUPER GOOD.
WHAT IS IT...STRAW-BERRY?
MAUREEN...I'M NOT KIDDING. I'M GOING TO TEAR YOU TO PIECES!
DON'T TOUCH MY MASCARA!
WHY NOT? THIS "MASK A RAT" IS SUPER.
OOOO! HERE'S SOME BASE... LOOOVE IT.
NOT MY FOUNDATION!
YOU DON'T EVEN KNOW HOW TO PUT IT ON.
SURE I DO. RIGHT ON MY FACE!
CAZENOVE/WILLIAM

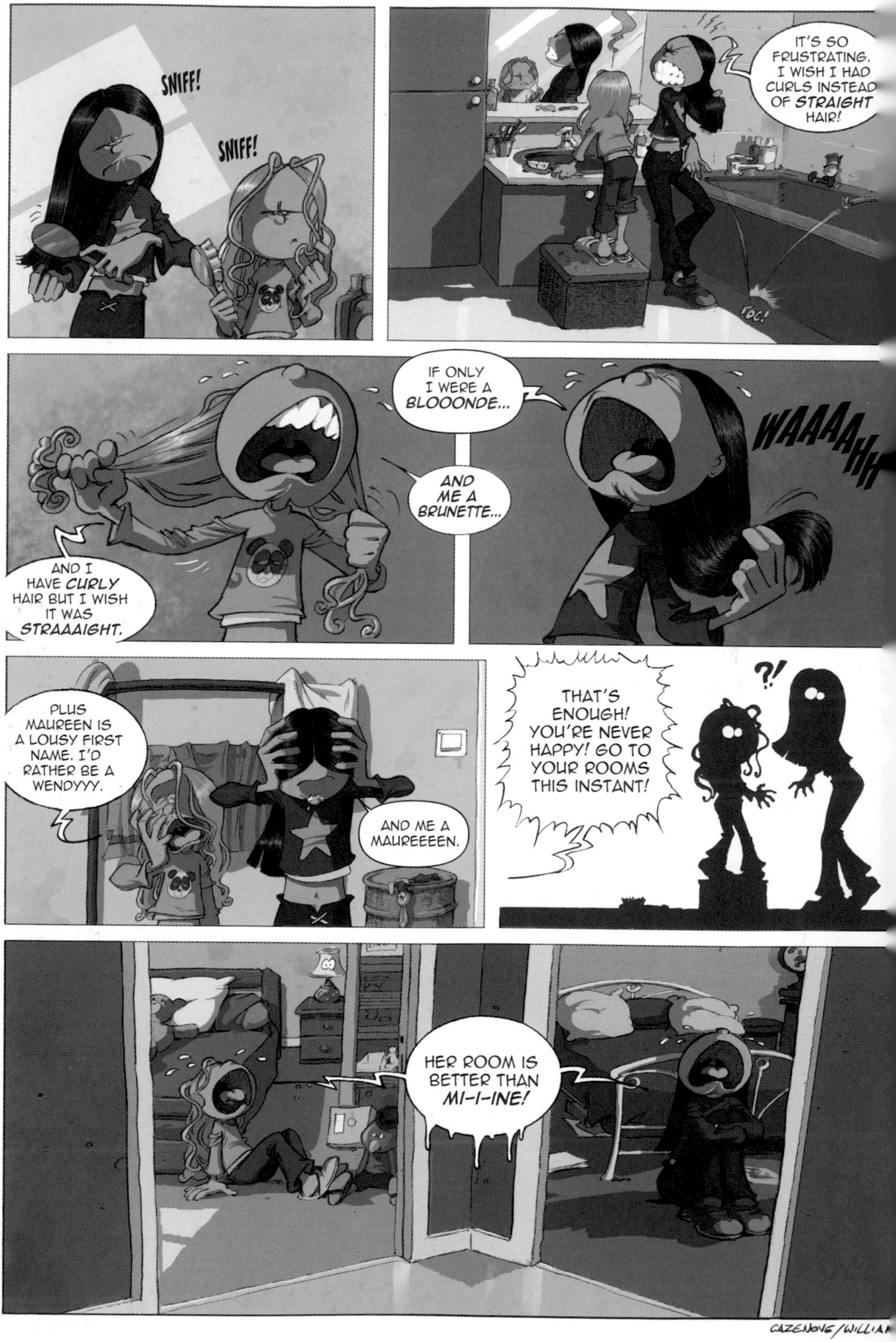
SNIFF!
SNIFF!
IT'S SO FRUSTRATING. I WISH I HAD CURLS INSTEAD OF STRAIGHT HAIR!
TOC!
IF ONLY I WERE A BLOOONDE...
AND ME A BRUNETTE...
AND I HAVE CURLY HAIR BUT I WISH IT WAS STRAAAIGHT.
WAAAAHH
PLUS MAUREEN IS A LOUSY FIRST NAME. I'D RATHER BE A WENDYYY.
AND ME A MAUREEEEN.
THAT'S ENOUGH! YOU'RE NEVER HAPPY! GO TO YOUR ROOMS THIS INSTANT!
?!
HER ROOM IS BETTER THAN MI-I-INE!
CAZENOVE/WILLIAM

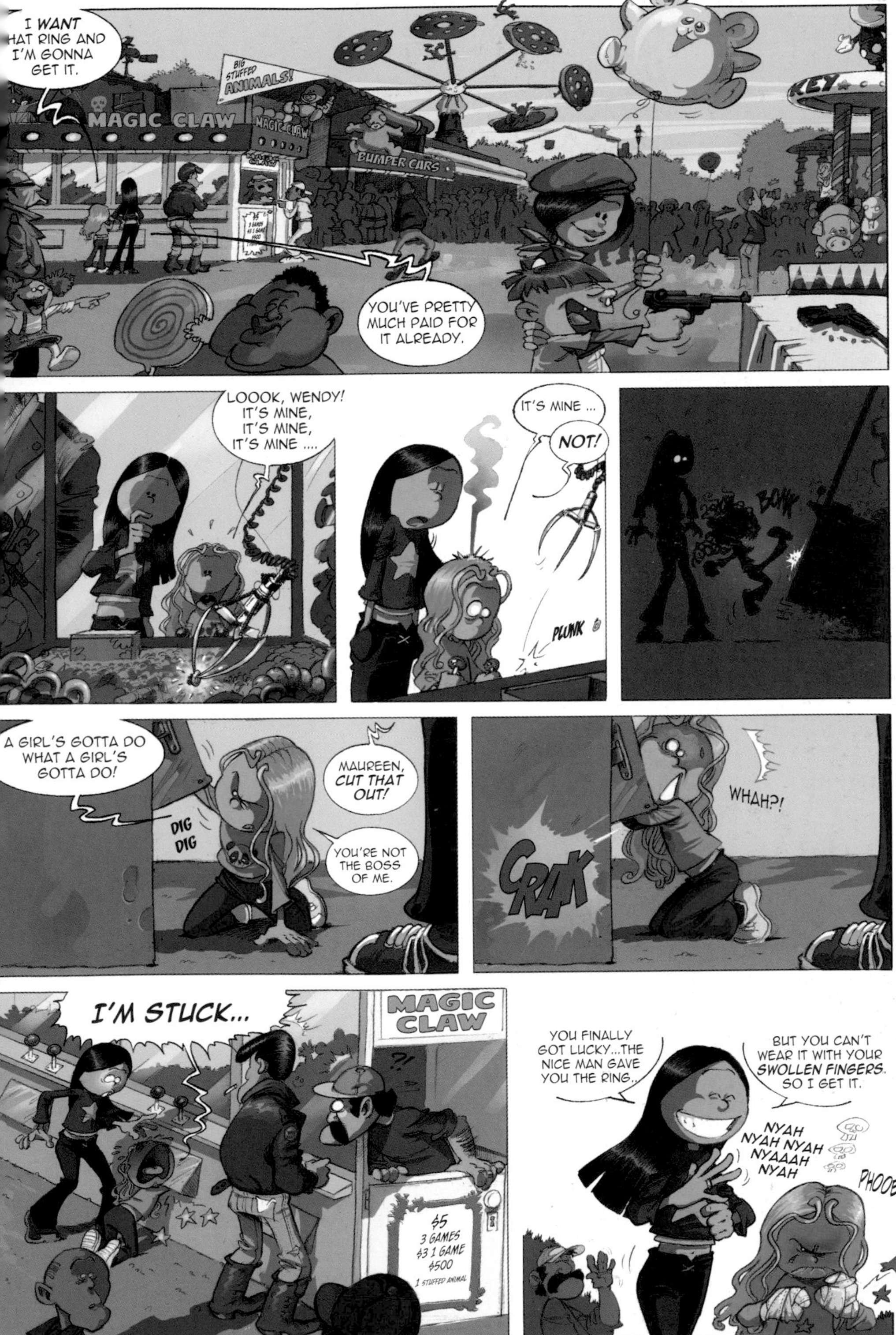
I WANT
HAT RING AND
I'M GONNA
GET IT.
MAGIC CLAW
BIG STUFFED ANIMALS!
BUMPER CARS
YOU'VE PRETTY
MUCH PAID FOR
IT ALREADY.
LOOOK, WENDY!
IT'S MINE,
IT'S MINE,
IT'S MINE ....
IT'S MINE ...
NOT!
PLUNK
BONK
A GIRL'S GOTTA DO
WHAT A GIRL'S
GOTTA DO!
DIG
DIG
MAUREEN,
CUT THAT
OUT!
YOU'RE NOT
THE BOSS
OF ME.
CRAK
WHAH?!
I'M STUCK...
MAGIC
CLAW
?!
$5
3 GAMES
$3 1 GAME
$500
1 STUFFED ANIMAL
YOU FINALLY
GOT LUCKY...THE
NICE MAN GAVE
YOU THE RING...
BUT YOU CAN'T
WEAR IT WITH YOUR
SWOLLEN FINGERS.
SO I GET IT.
NYAH
NYAH NYAH
NYAAAH
NYAH
PHOOEY!
CAZENOVE/WILLIAM

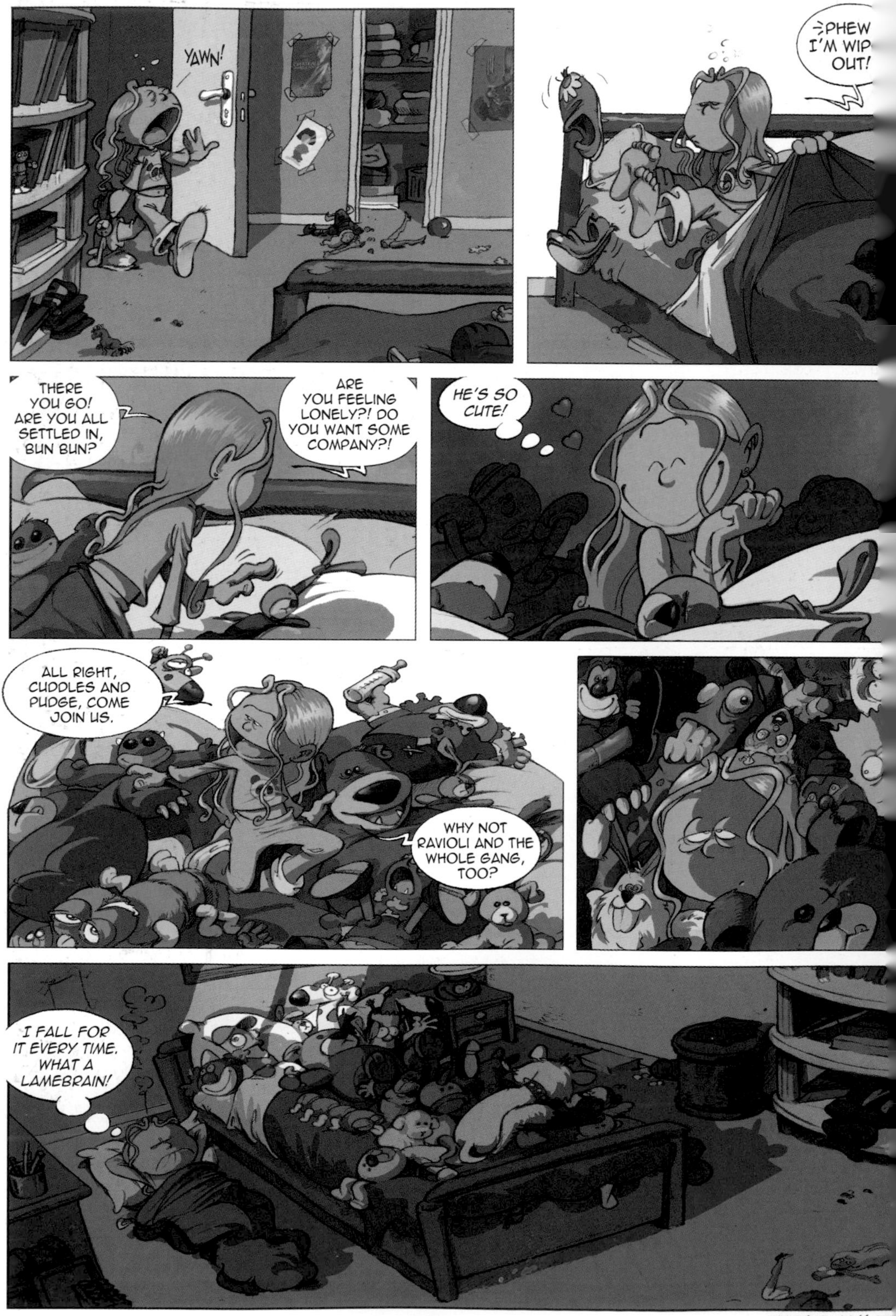
YAWN!
PHEW I'M WIP OUT!
THERE YOU GO! ARE YOU ALL SETTLED IN, BUN BUN?
ARE YOU FEELING LONELY?! DO YOU WANT SOME COMPANY?!
HE'S SO CUTE!
ALL RIGHT, CUDDLES AND PUDGE, COME JOIN US.
WHY NOT RAVIOLI AND THE WHOLE GANG, TOO?
I FALL FOR IT EVERY TIME. WHAT A LAMEBRAIN!
CAZENOVE/WILLIAM

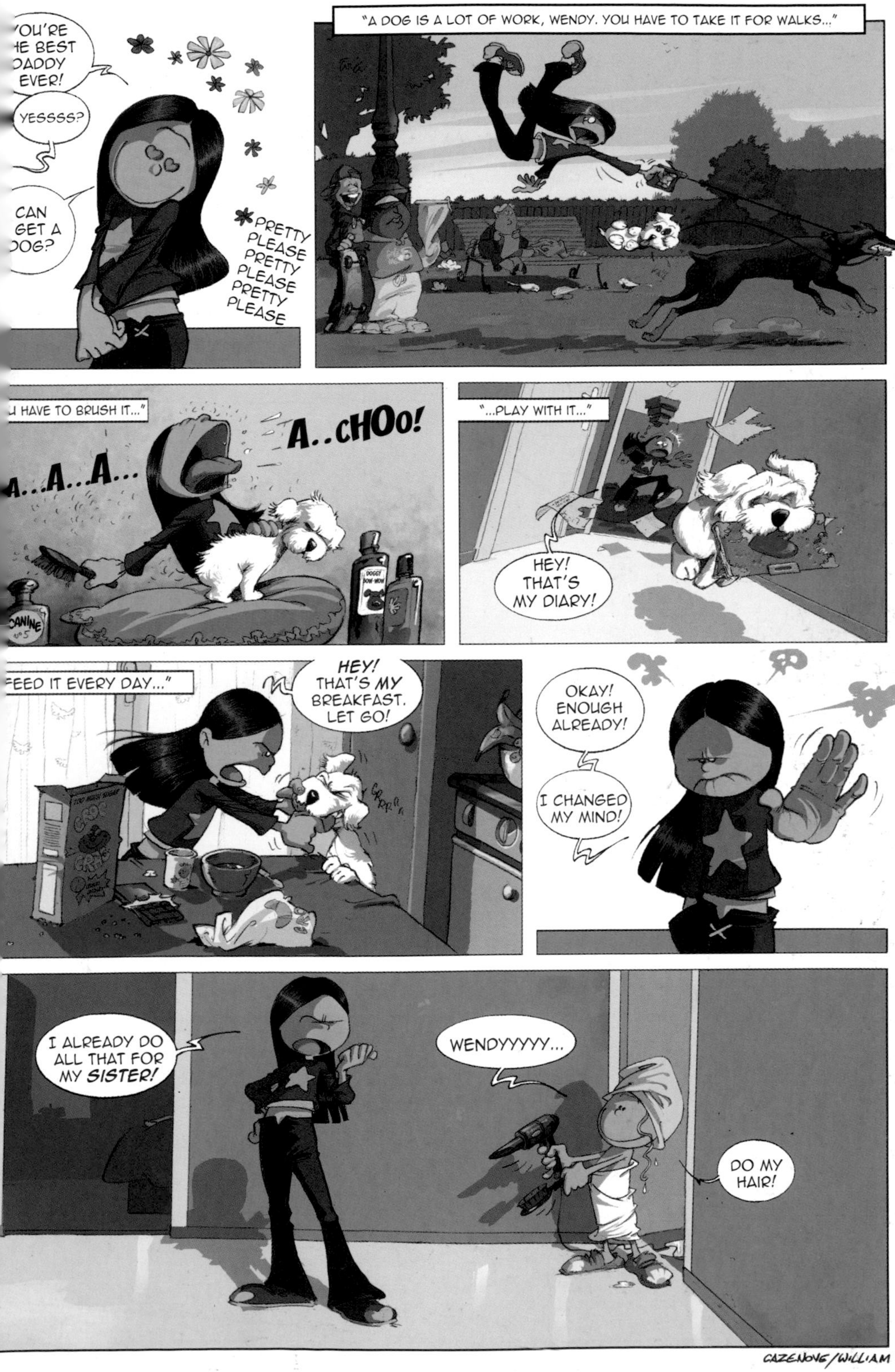
OU'RE HE BEST DADDY EVER!
YESSSS?
CAN GET A OG?
PRETTY PLEASE PRETTY PLEASE PRETTY PLEASE
"A DOG IS A LOT OF WORK, WENDY. YOU HAVE TO TAKE IT FOR WALKS..."
U HAVE TO BRUSH IT..."
A...A...A...
A..CHOo!
DOGGY BOW-WOW
CANINE Nº5
"...PLAY WITH IT..."
HEY! THAT'S MY DIARY!
FEED IT EVERY DAY..."
HEY! THAT'S MY BREAKFAST. LET GO!
GRRR
OKAY! ENOUGH ALREADY!
I CHANGED MY MIND!
I ALREADY DO ALL THAT FOR MY SISTER!
WENDYYYYY...
DO MY HAIR!
CAZENOVE/WILLIAM

Don't miss THE SISTERS #1 "Just Like Family" – Coming Soon!

WATCH OUT FOR PAPERCUTZ

Welcome to the togetherness-themed third DISNEY GRAPHIC NOVELS graphic novel—otherwise knc as the fabulous first MINNIE & DAISY graphic novel—from Papercutz, those funny humans devotec publishing great graphic novels for all ages. I'm Jim Salicrup, the Papercutz Editor-in-Chief and frequ visitor to the Happiest Place on Earth!

But wait, you may be wondering, what's all this about MINNIE & DAISY being the third Disney grap novel from Papercutz? Well, to avoid further confusion, let's just say that Papercutz started publish Disney graphic novels years ago with DISNEY FAIRIES—that wonderful series starring Tinker Bell and fairy friends from Pixie Hollow. DISNEY FAIRIES continues to be published by Papercutz, but we th added a series with the title DISNEY GRAPHIC NOVELS, and the tricky part is that it's actually f Disney graphic novel series in one! The first volume featured a comics adaptation of DISNEY PLANES, second volume included the American debut of DISNEY X-MICKEY, the supernatural adventures Mickey Mouse, and the third volume—this volume—collects DISNEY MINNIE & DAISY comics. There! hope that clears up any confusion, but even if it doesn't—don't worry! Just enjoy the comics!

And what delightful comics they are! Not only do we get to have a lot of fun with Minnie & Daisy, b we're also getting to meet their friends and neighbors. We also explore various interesting parts Minnie & Daisy's lives, and I suspect there's even more to come in future MINNIE & DAISY graphic nove

While enjoying the adventures of MINNIE & DAISY myself, I couldn't help thinking that these Best Frier Forever are a lot like sisters, and that reminded me of another exciting new graphic novel series Paperc is publishing—THE SISTERS! The title says it all—it's about bigger sister Wendy and little sister Mauree Like most sisters, they love each other a lot, but they tend to disagree about almost everything. They manage to work things out, but at times it seems like a never-ending battle. To give you and even bet idea what THE SISTERS are all about, we're including a short preview in this very graphic novel. We hop you enjoy it, and pick up THE SISTERS #1 "Just Like Family," available at your favorite bookseller.

Now, I'm betting those of you who paid really close attention to the second paragraph, a wondering, what's the fourth of the four DISNEY GRAPHIC NOVELS series? There's DISNEY PLANE DISNEY X-MICKEY, and DISNEY MINNIE & DAISY—that just adds up to three! You are correct! The four series is really something different. Imagine if Disney poked a little fun at some of the greatest stori ever told-- and recast these classics with such Disney stars as Mickey Mouse, Minnie Mouse, Dona Duck, Huey, Dewy, and Louie, Dumbo, even Doc and Dopey from the Seven Dwarves and many mor That's what DISNEY GREAT PARODIES will be, starting with "Mickey's Inferno." And it's coming soon!

So, speaking of Mickey Mouse, what better way to end this "Watch Out for Papercutz" page than th closing lyrics to the original Mickey Mouse Club...

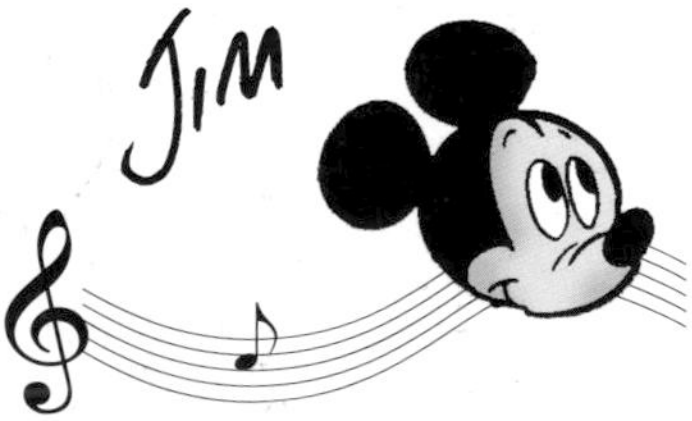
JIM

"Now it's time to say goodbye/ To all our company/ M-I-C, (See you real soon) K-E-Y, (Why? Because we like you!) M-O-U-S-E"!

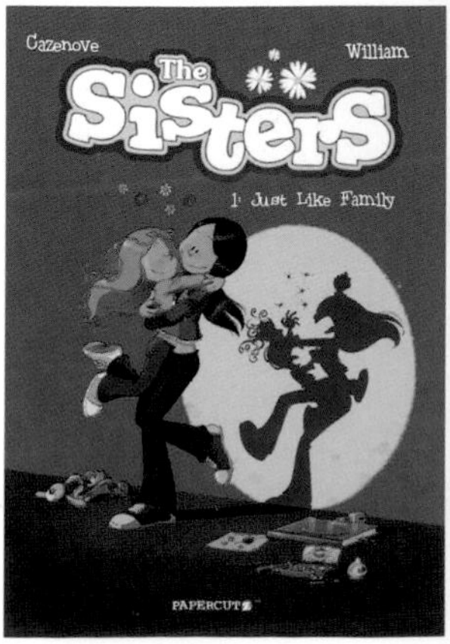
Cazenove
William
The Sisters
1: Just Like Family
PAPERCUTZ

STAY IN TOUCH!

EMAIL:	salicrup@papercutz.com
WEB:	papercutz.com
TWITTER:	@papercutzgn
FACEBOOK:	PAPERCUTZGRAPHICNOVELS
FAN MAIL:	Papercutz, 160 Broadway, Suite 700, East Wing, New York, NY 10038

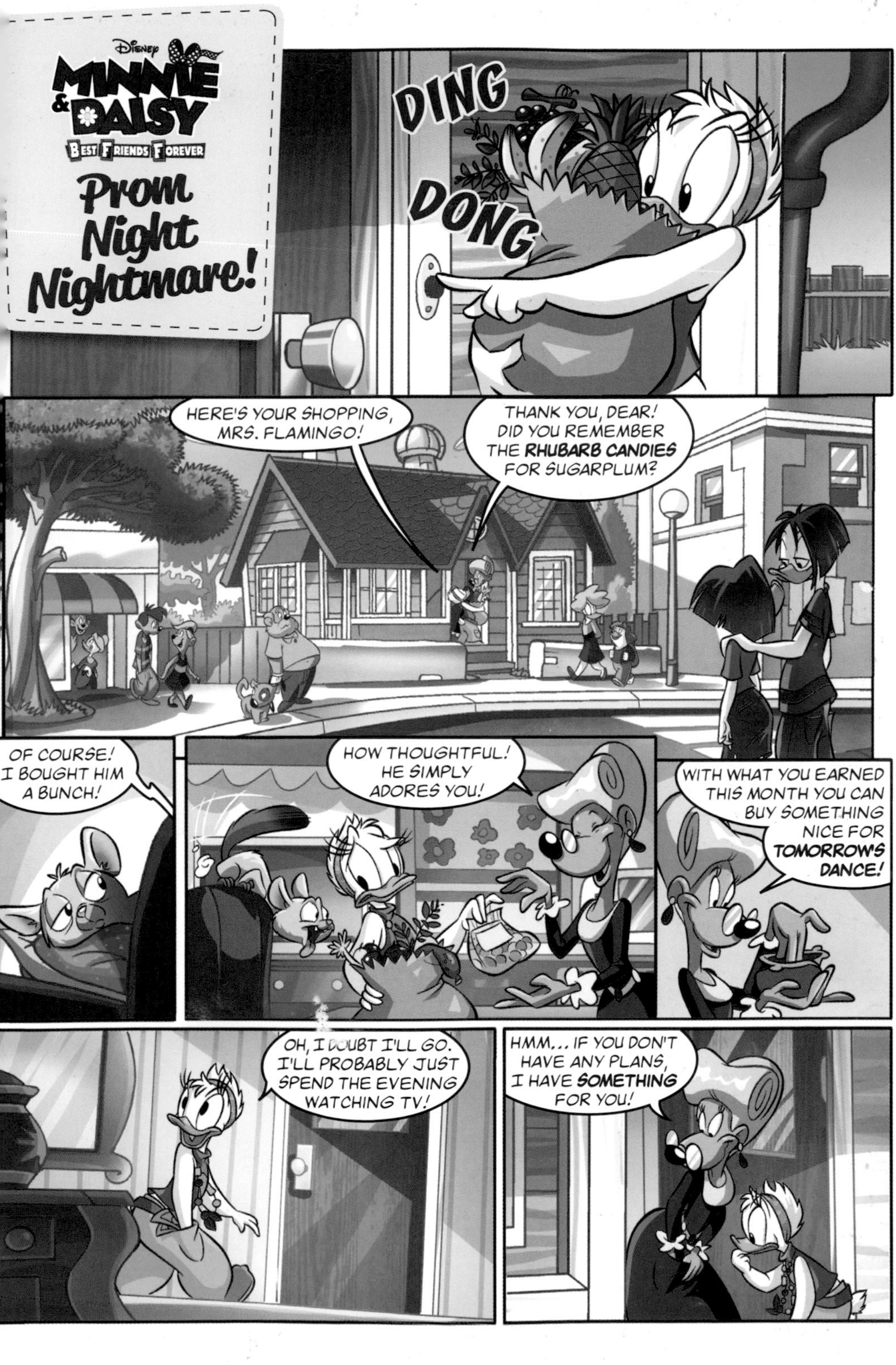
DISNEY
MINNIE & DAISY
BEST FRIENDS FOREVER
Prom Night Nightmare!
DING
DONG
HERE'S YOUR SHOPPING, MRS. FLAMINGO!
THANK YOU, DEAR! DID YOU REMEMBER THE RHUBARB CANDIES FOR SUGARPLUM?
OF COURSE! I BOUGHT HIM A BUNCH!
HOW THOUGHTFUL! HE SIMPLY ADORES YOU!
WITH WHAT YOU EARNED THIS MONTH YOU CAN BUY SOMETHING NICE FOR TOMORROW'S DANCE!
OH, I DOUBT I'LL GO. I'LL PROBABLY JUST SPEND THE EVENING WATCHING TV!
HMM... IF YOU DON'T HAVE ANY PLANS, I HAVE SOMETHING FOR YOU!

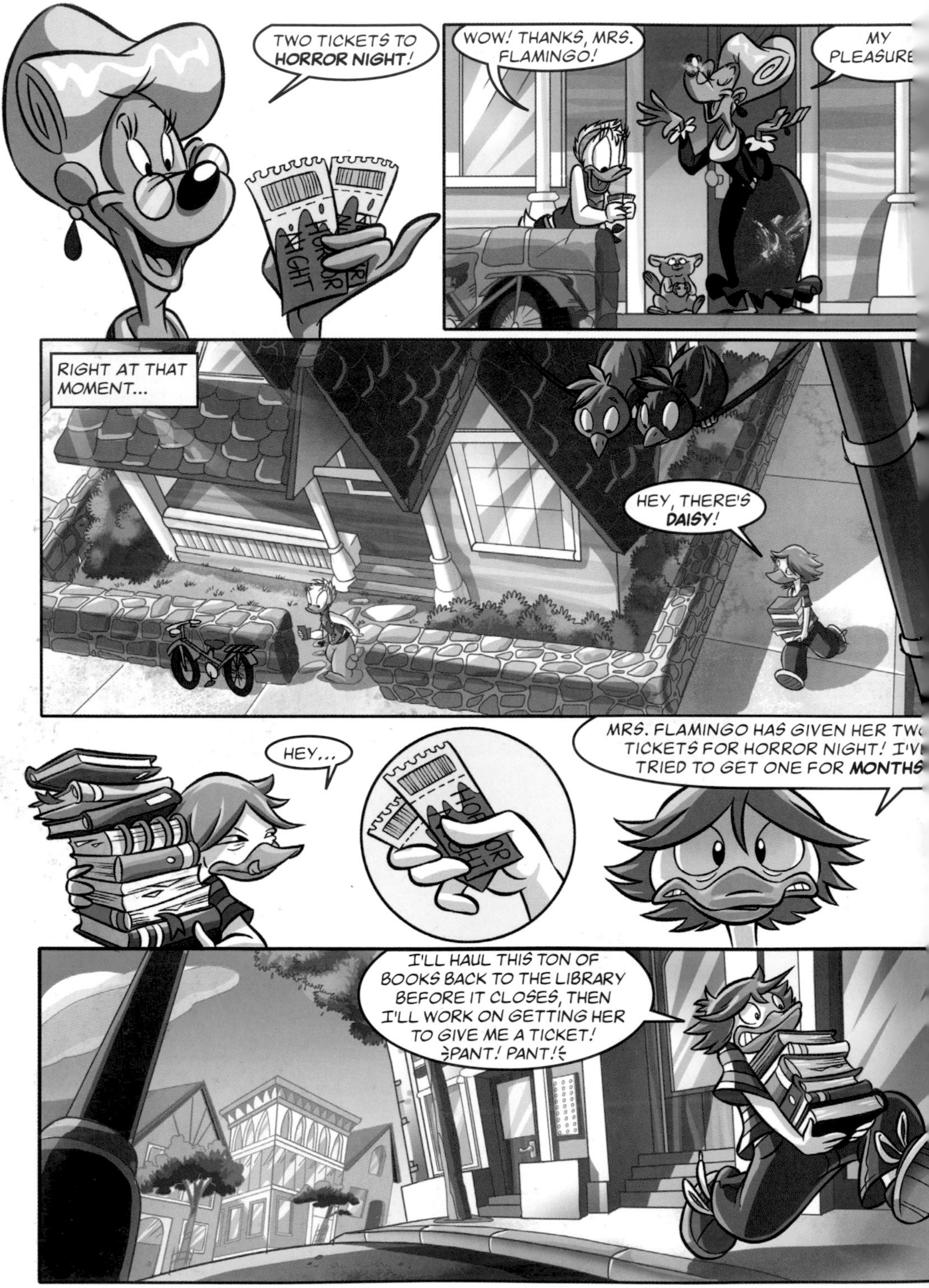
TWO TICKETS TO HORROR NIGHT!
HORROR NIGHT
WOW! THANKS, MRS. FLAMINGO!
MY PLEASURE
RIGHT AT THAT MOMENT...
HEY, THERE'S DAISY!
HEY...
MRS. FLAMINGO HAS GIVEN HER TWO TICKETS FOR HORROR NIGHT! I'VE TRIED TO GET ONE FOR MONTHS
I'LL HAUL THIS TON OF BOOKS BACK TO THE LIBRARY BEFORE IT CLOSES, THEN I'LL WORK ON GETTING HER TO GIVE ME A TICKET! PANT! PANT!

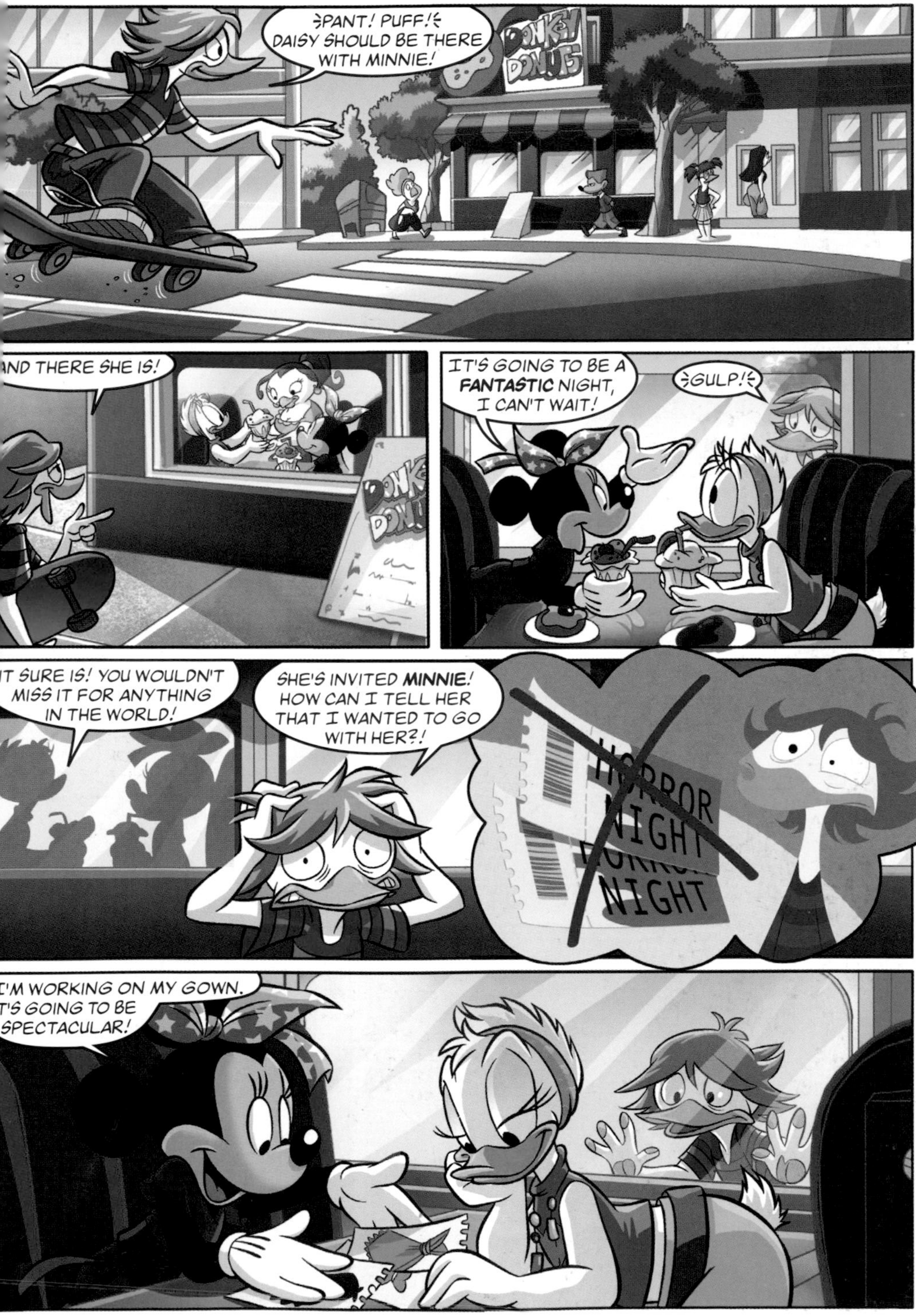

⋟PANT! PUFF!⋞ DAISY SHOULD BE THERE WITH MINNIE!
DONKEY DONUTS
AND THERE SHE IS!
IT'S GOING TO BE A FANTASTIC NIGHT, I CAN'T WAIT!
⋟GULP!⋞
IT SURE IS! YOU WOULDN'T MISS IT FOR ANYTHING IN THE WORLD!
SHE'S INVITED MINNIE! HOW CAN I TELL HER THAT I WANTED TO GO WITH HER?!
HORROR NIGHT
NIGHT
I'M WORKING ON MY GOWN. IT'S GOING TO BE SPECTACULAR!

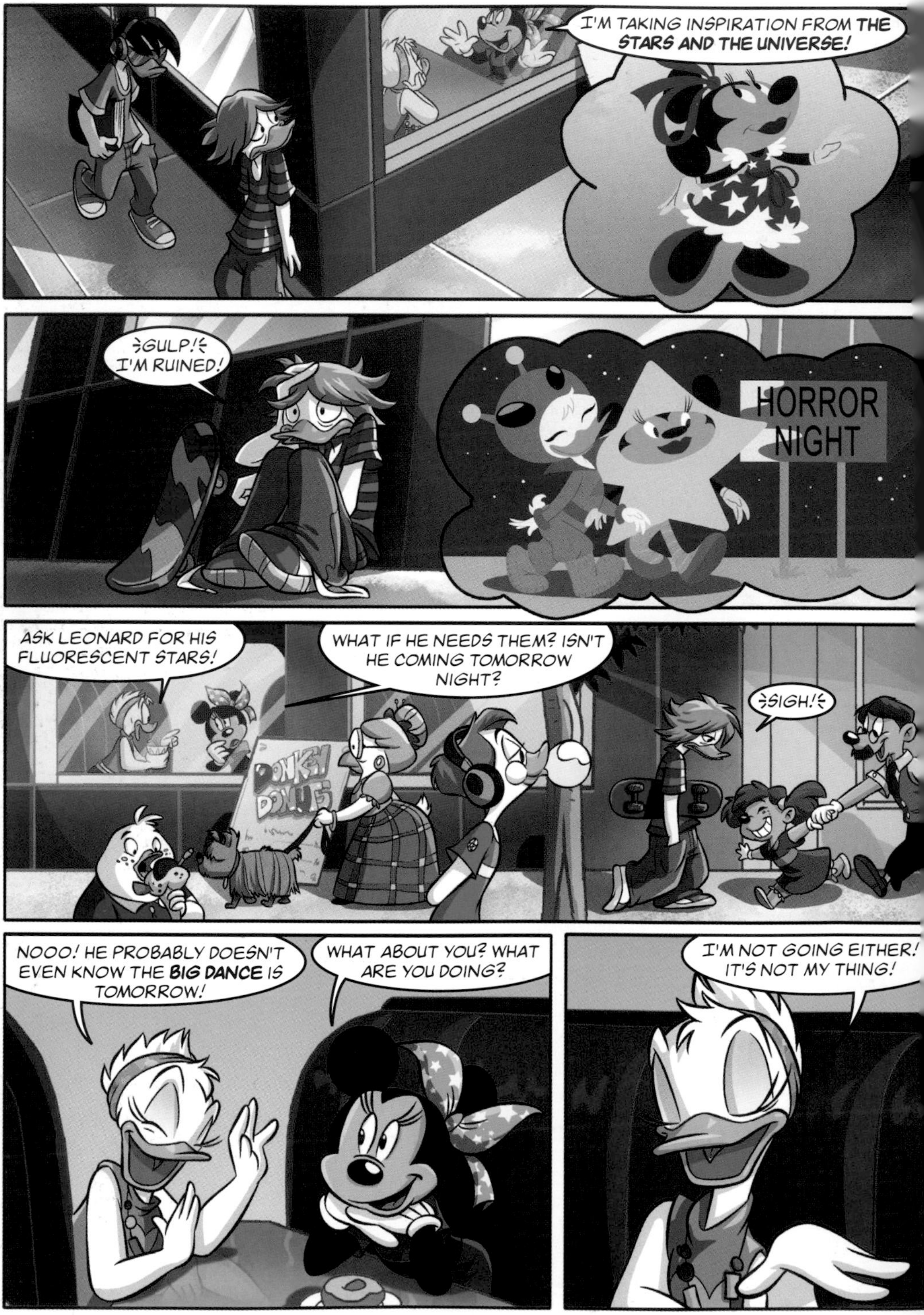
I'M TAKING INSPIRATION FROM THE STARS AND THE UNIVERSE!
GULP! I'M RUINED!
HORROR NIGHT
ASK LEONARD FOR HIS FLUORESCENT STARS!
WHAT IF HE NEEDS THEM? ISN'T HE COMING TOMORROW NIGHT?
DONKEY DONUTS
SIGH!
NOOO! HE PROBABLY DOESN'T EVEN KNOW THE BIG DANCE IS TOMORROW!
WHAT ABOUT YOU? WHAT ARE YOU DOING?
I'M NOT GOING EITHER! IT'S NOT MY THING!

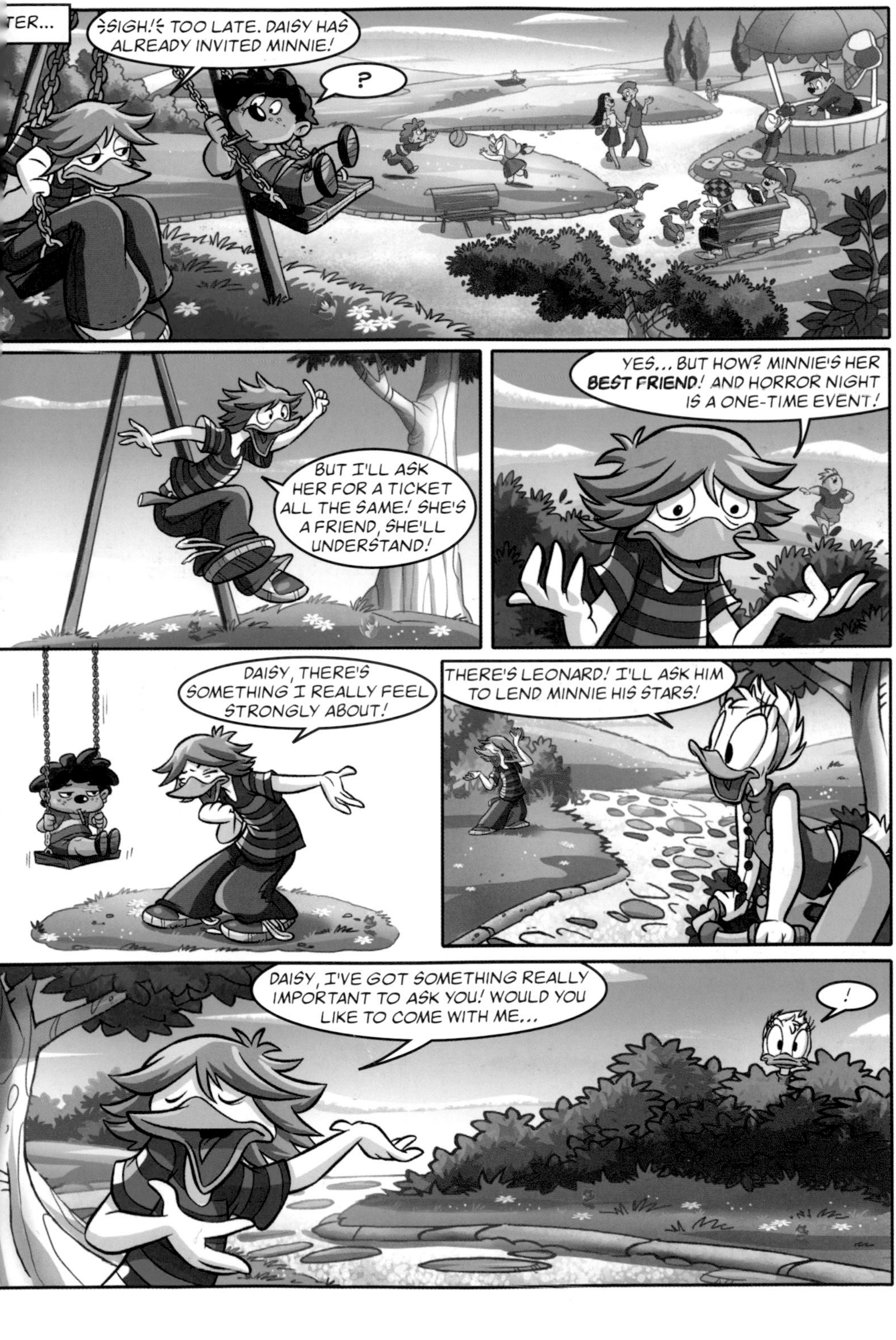
TER...
¿SIGH!¿ TOO LATE. DAISY HAS ALREADY INVITED MINNIE!
?
BUT I'LL ASK HER FOR A TICKET ALL THE SAME! SHE'S A FRIEND, SHE'LL UNDERSTAND!
YES... BUT HOW? MINNIE'S HER BEST FRIEND! AND HORROR NIGHT IS A ONE-TIME EVENT!
DAISY, THERE'S SOMETHING I REALLY FEEL STRONGLY ABOUT!
THERE'S LEONARD! I'LL ASK HIM TO LEND MINNIE HIS STARS!
DAISY, I'VE GOT SOMETHING REALLY IMPORTANT TO ASK YOU! WOULD YOU LIKE TO COME WITH ME...
!

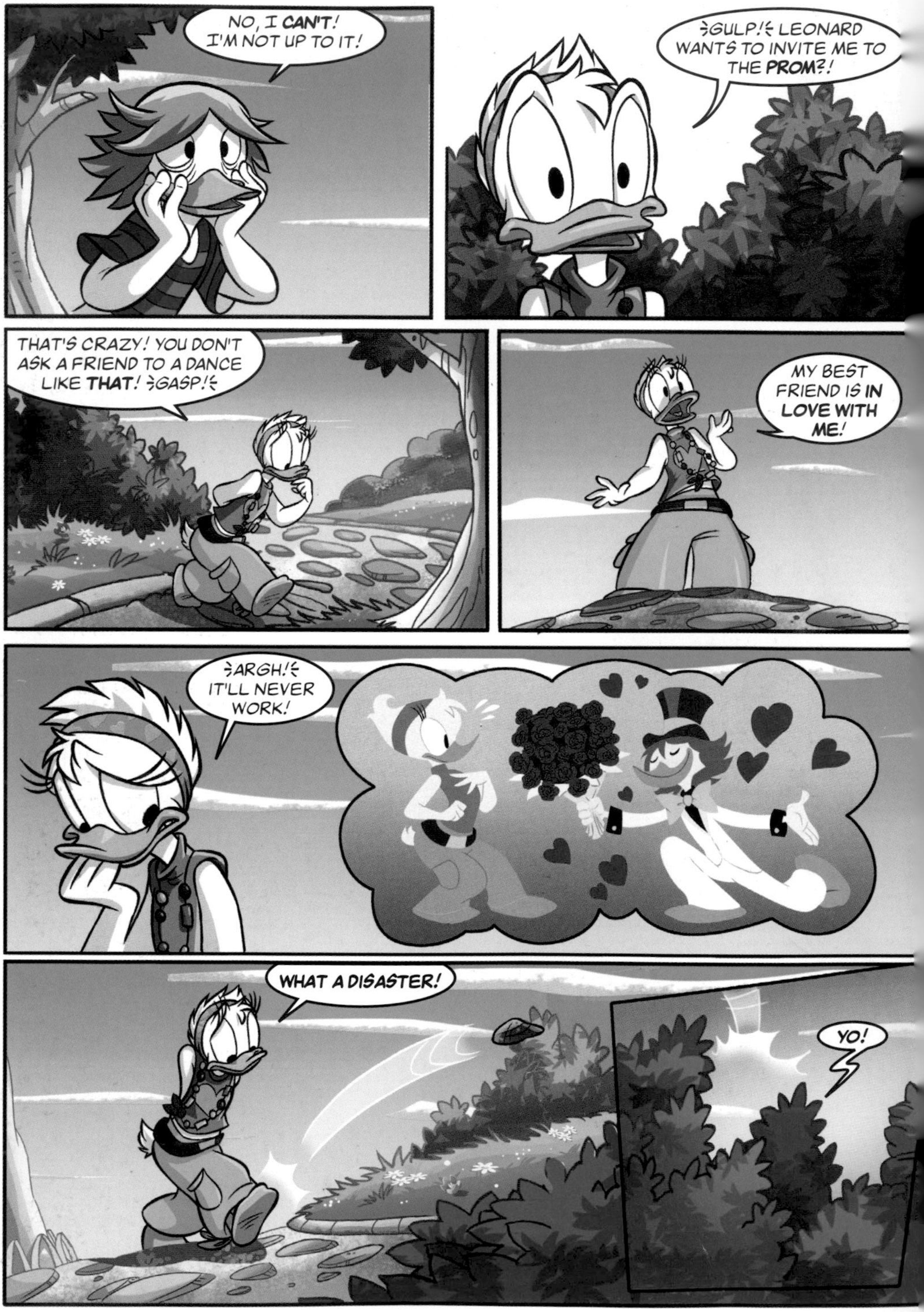
NO, I CAN'T! I'M NOT UP TO IT!
⁝GULP!⁝ LEONARD WANTS TO INVITE ME TO THE PROM?!
THAT'S CRAZY! YOU DON'T ASK A FRIEND TO A DANCE LIKE THAT! ⁝GASP!⁝
MY BEST FRIEND IS IN LOVE WITH ME!
⁝ARGH!⁝ IT'LL NEVER WORK!
WHAT A DISASTER!
YO!

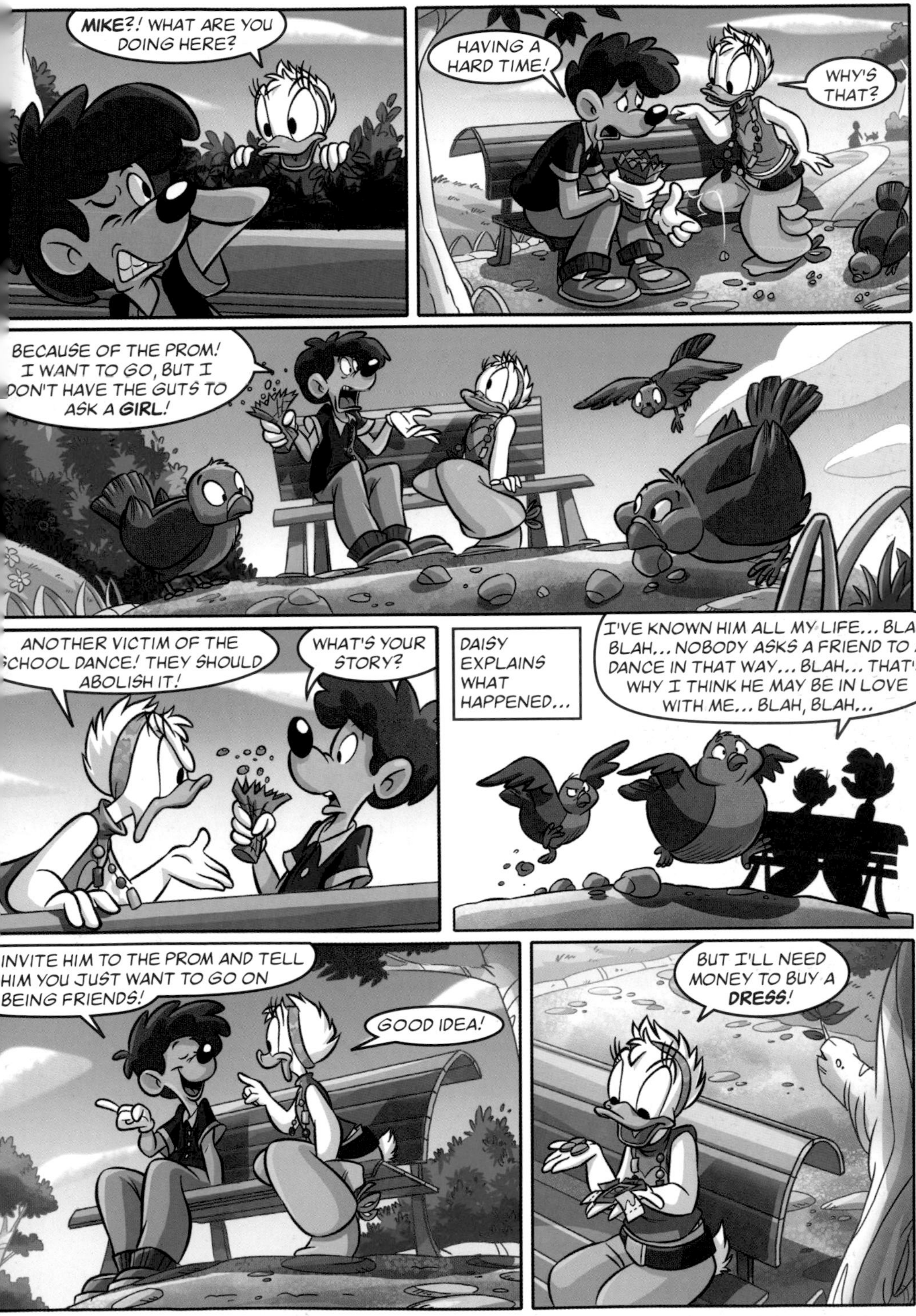

MIKE?! WHAT ARE YOU DOING HERE?
HAVING A HARD TIME!
WHY'S THAT?
BECAUSE OF THE PROM! I WANT TO GO, BUT I DON'T HAVE THE GUTS TO ASK A GIRL!
ANOTHER VICTIM OF THE SCHOOL DANCE! THEY SHOULD ABOLISH IT!
WHAT'S YOUR STORY?
DAISY EXPLAINS WHAT HAPPENED...
I'VE KNOWN HIM ALL MY LIFE... BLAH, BLAH... NOBODY ASKS A FRIEND TO A DANCE IN THAT WAY... BLAH... THAT'S WHY I THINK HE MAY BE IN LOVE WITH ME... BLAH, BLAH...
INVITE HIM TO THE PROM AND TELL HIM YOU JUST WANT TO GO ON BEING FRIENDS!
GOOD IDEA!
BUT I'LL NEED MONEY TO BUY A DRESS!

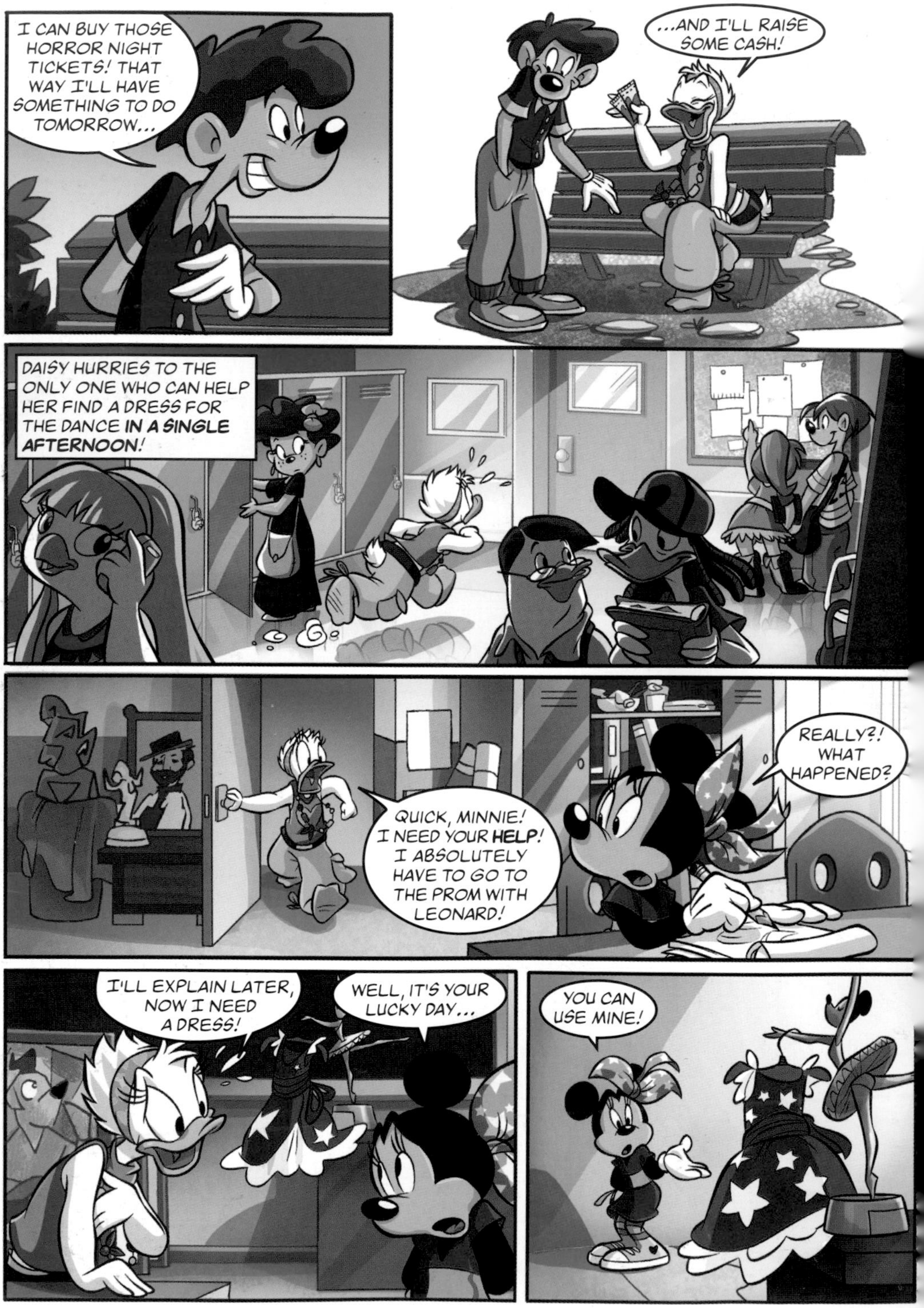
I CAN BUY THOSE HORROR NIGHT TICKETS! THAT WAY I'LL HAVE SOMETHING TO DO TOMORROW...
...AND I'LL RAISE SOME CASH!
DAISY HURRIES TO THE ONLY ONE WHO CAN HELP HER FIND A DRESS FOR THE DANCE **IN A SINGLE AFTERNOON**!
QUICK, MINNIE! I NEED YOUR **HELP**! I ABSOLUTELY HAVE TO GO TO THE PROM WITH LEONARD!
REALLY?! WHAT HAPPENED?
I'LL EXPLAIN LATER, NOW I NEED A DRESS!
WELL, IT'S YOUR LUCKY DAY...
YOU CAN USE MINE!

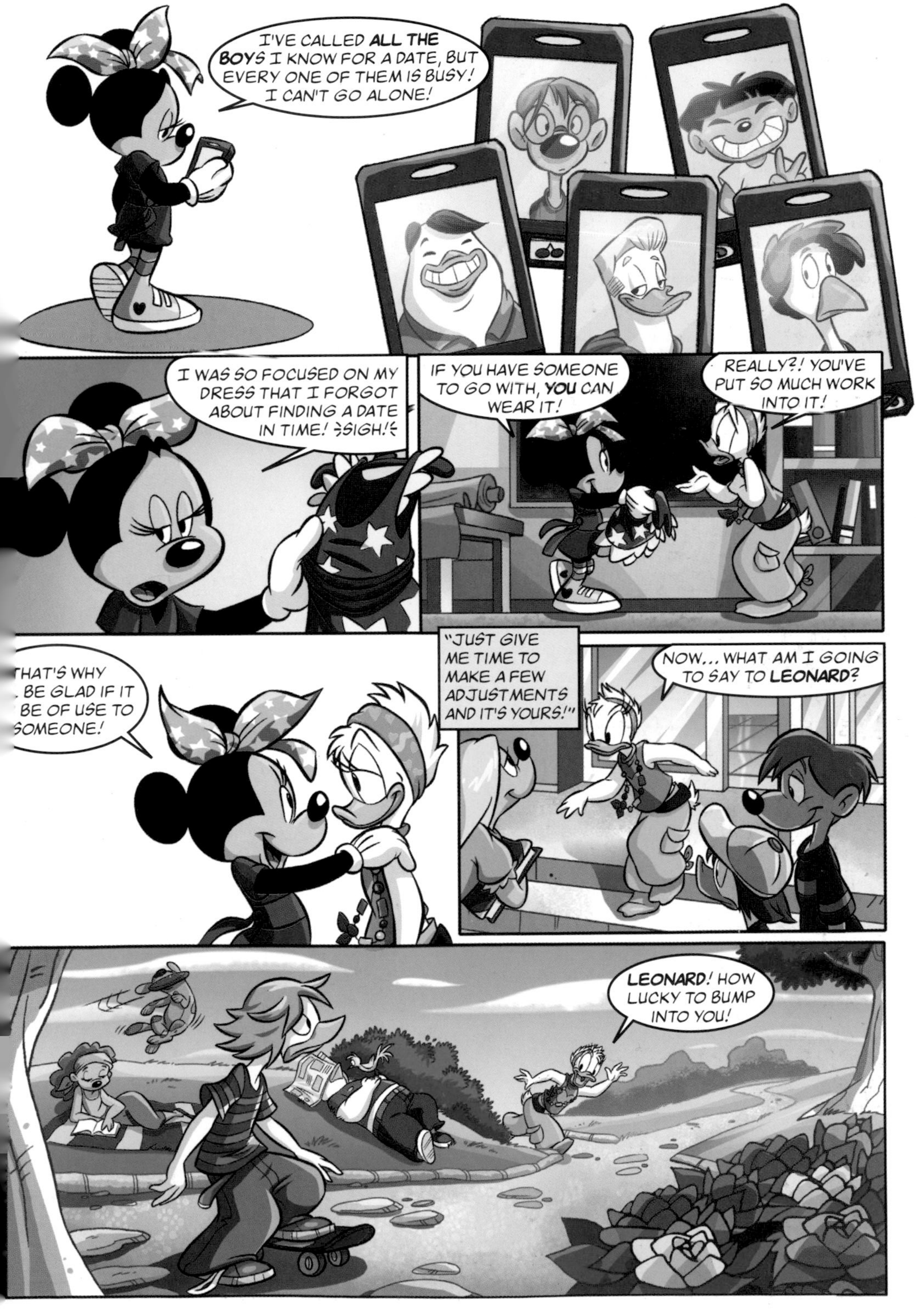
I'VE CALLED ALL THE BOYS I KNOW FOR A DATE, BUT EVERY ONE OF THEM IS BUSY! I CAN'T GO ALONE!
I WAS SO FOCUSED ON MY DRESS THAT I FORGOT ABOUT FINDING A DATE IN TIME! SIGH!
IF YOU HAVE SOMEONE TO GO WITH, YOU CAN WEAR IT!
REALLY?! YOU'VE PUT SO MUCH WORK INTO IT!
THAT'S WHY
BE GLAD IF IT
BE OF USE TO
SOMEONE!
"JUST GIVE ME TIME TO MAKE A FEW ADJUSTMENTS AND IT'S YOURS!"
NOW... WHAT AM I GOING TO SAY TO LEONARD?
LEONARD! HOW LUCKY TO BUMP INTO YOU!

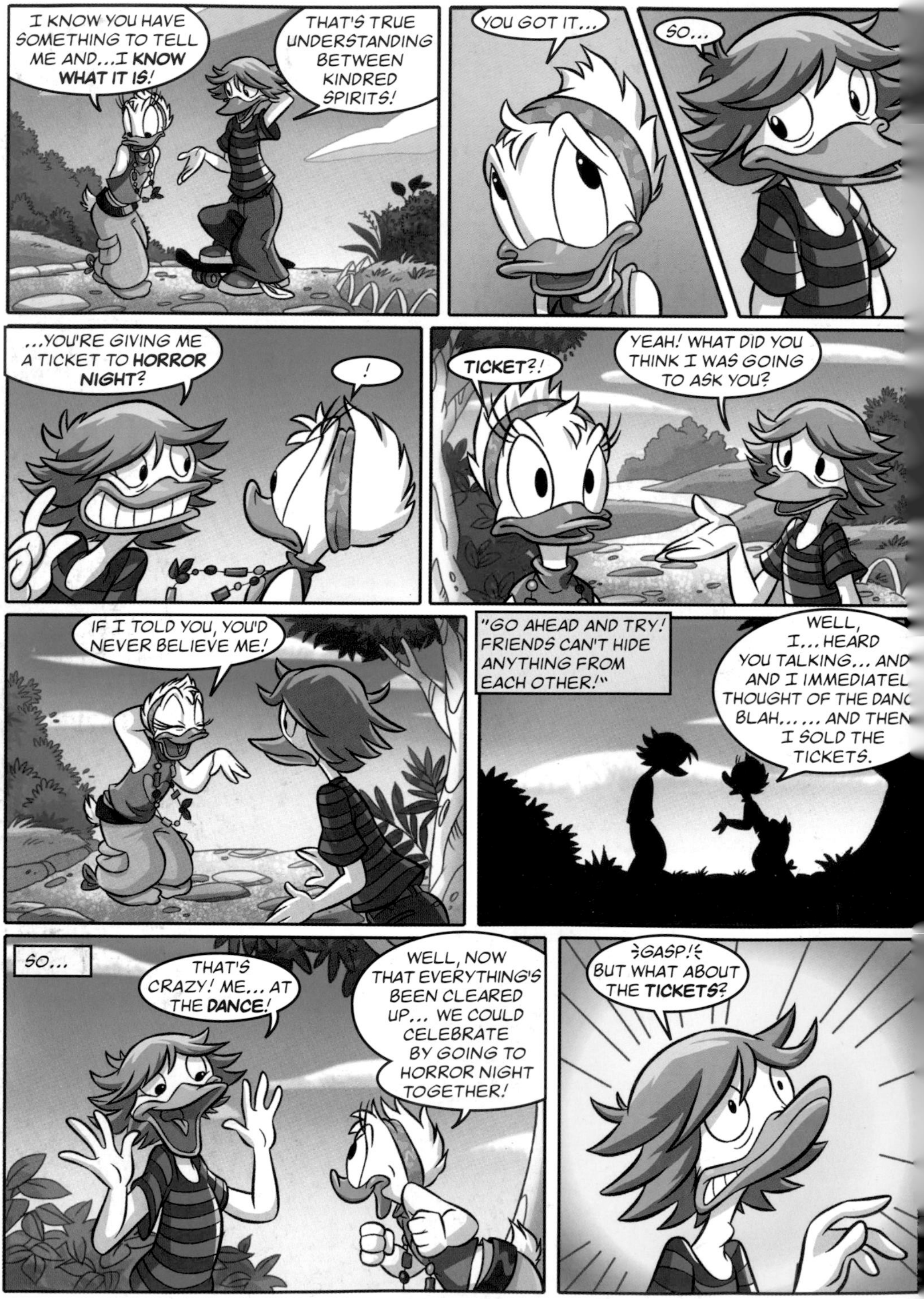
I KNOW YOU HAVE SOMETHING TO TELL ME AND...I KNOW WHAT IT IS!
THAT'S TRUE UNDERSTANDING BETWEEN KINDRED SPIRITS!
YOU GOT IT...
SO...
...YOU'RE GIVING ME A TICKET TO HORROR NIGHT?
!
TICKET?!
YEAH! WHAT DID YOU THINK I WAS GOING TO ASK YOU?
IF I TOLD YOU, YOU'D NEVER BELIEVE ME!
"GO AHEAD AND TRY! FRIENDS CAN'T HIDE ANYTHING FROM EACH OTHER!"
WELL, I... HEARD YOU TALKING... AND AND I IMMEDIATEL THOUGHT OF THE DANC BLAH...... AND THEN I SOLD THE TICKETS.
SO...
THAT'S CRAZY! ME... AT THE DANCE!
WELL, NOW THAT EVERYTHING'S BEEN CLEARED UP... WE COULD CELEBRATE BY GOING TO HORROR NIGHT TOGETHER!
GASP! BUT WHAT ABOUT THE TICKETS?

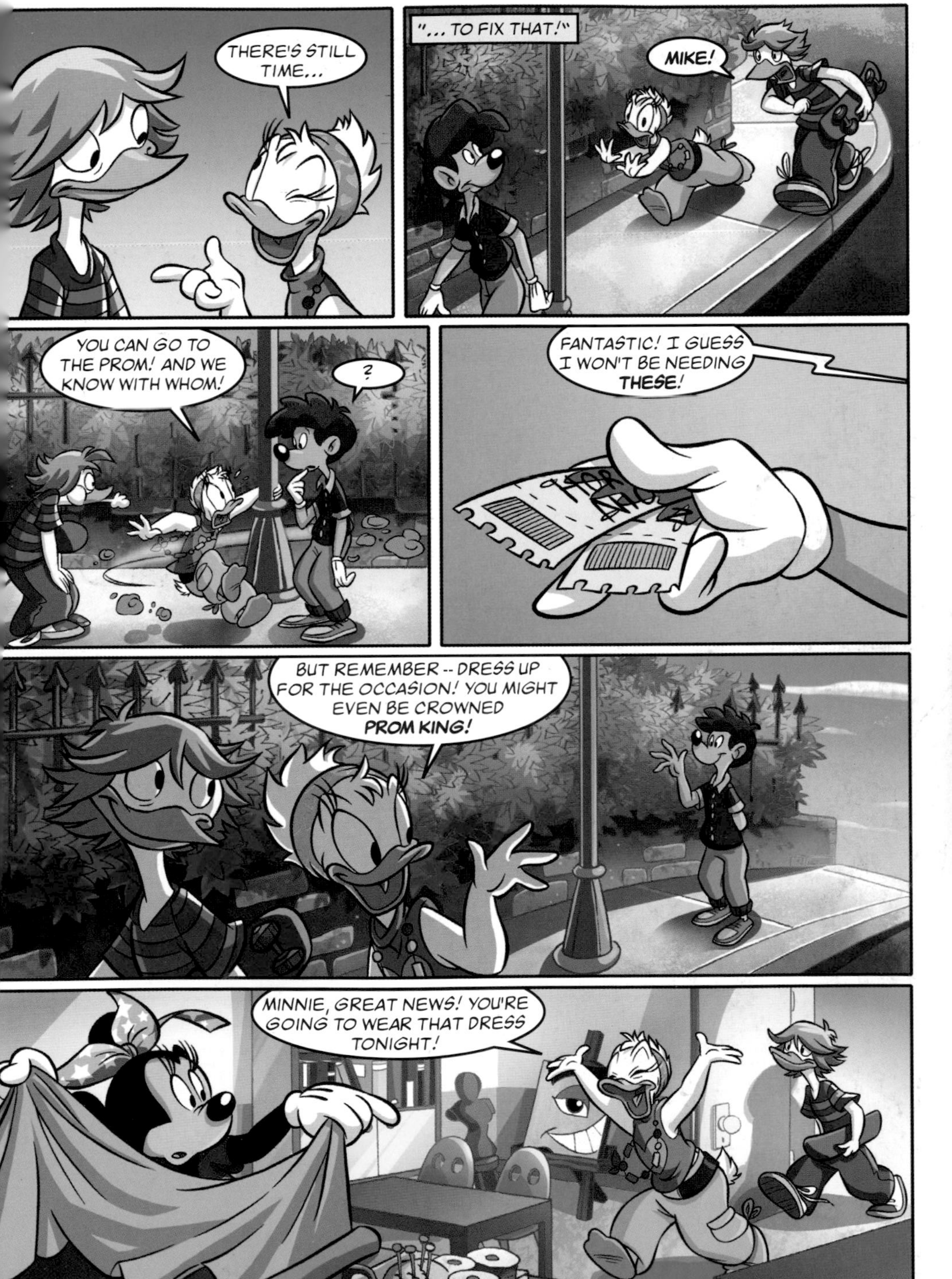
THERE'S STILL TIME...
"...TO FIX THAT!"
MIKE!
YOU CAN GO TO THE PROM! AND WE KNOW WITH WHOM!
?
FANTASTIC! I GUESS I WON'T BE NEEDING THESE!
BUT REMEMBER -- DRESS UP FOR THE OCCASION! YOU MIGHT EVEN BE CROWNED PROM KING!
MINNIE, GREAT NEWS! YOU'RE GOING TO WEAR THAT DRESS TONIGHT!

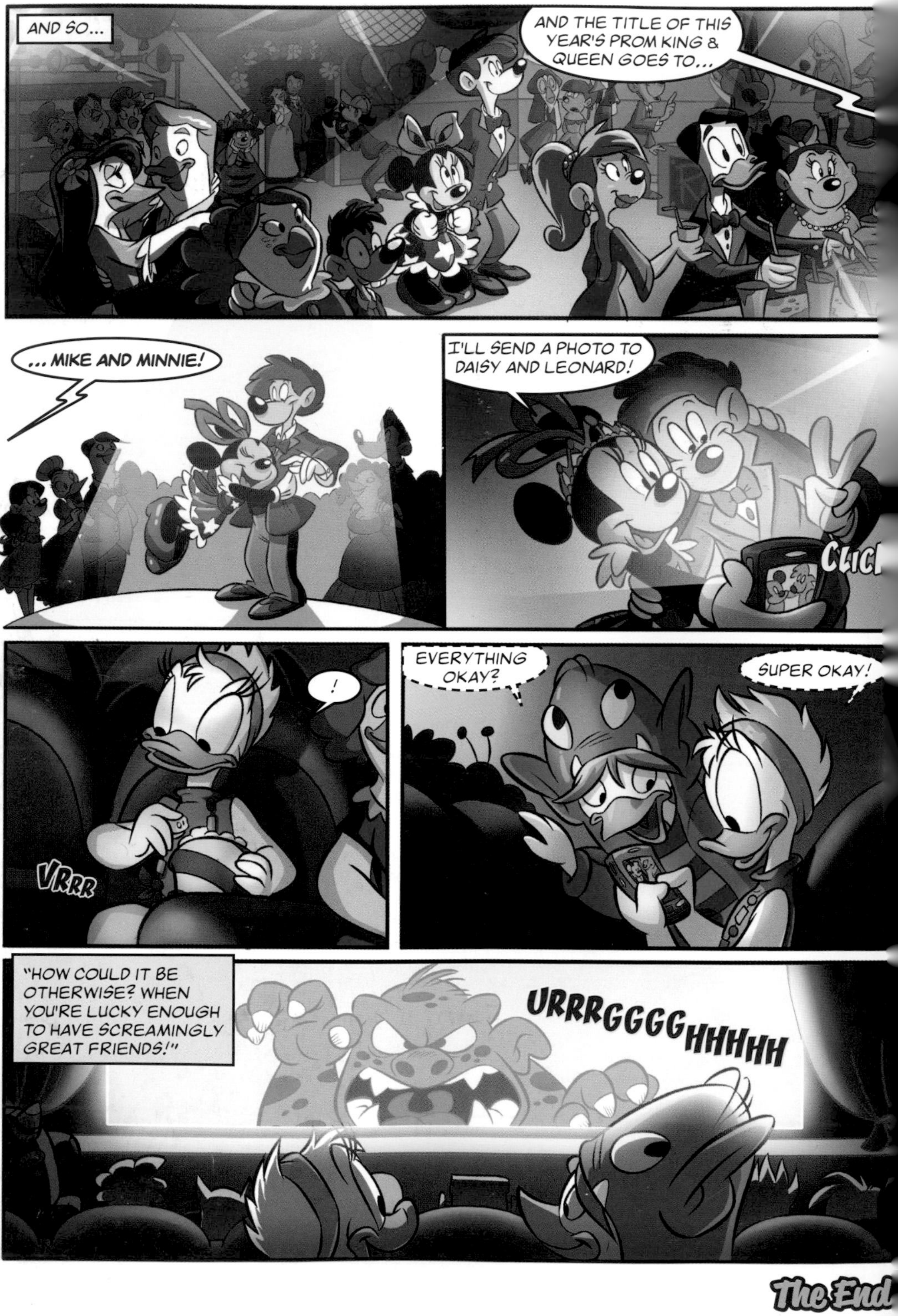
AND SO...
AND THE TITLE OF THIS YEAR'S PROM KING & QUEEN GOES TO...
...MIKE AND MINNIE!
I'LL SEND A PHOTO TO DAISY AND LEONARD!
CLICK
!
VRRR
EVERYTHING OKAY?
SUPER OKAY!
"HOW COULD IT BE OTHERWISE? WHEN YOU'RE LUCKY ENOUGH TO HAVE SCREAMINGLY GREAT FRIENDS!"
URRRGGGGHHHHH
The End